Cheryl Bolduc A-7

St. Louis And The Last Crusade

ST. LOUIS AND
THE LAST CRUSADE

by
Margaret Ann
Hubbard

illustrated by
Harry Barton

Farrar, Straus & Cudahy
Burns & Oates

VISION BOOKS
New York
London

VISION BOOKS
IS A DIVISION OF
FARRAR, STRAUS & CUDAHY, INC.
PUBLISHED SIMULTANEOUSLY IN CANADA BY
AMBASSADOR BOOKS, LTD., TORONTO.
MANUFACTURED IN THE U.S.A.

For Jeannie, Dickie and Kathy Priley.

Contents

Author's Note

If ever there was a storybook character in real life, it was Louis IX of France. In writing about him an author is confronted with only one difficulty: which incidents shall be used out of a lifetime teeming with adventure and accomplishment. When space is limited, many interesting episodes must be omitted. I have tried, therefore, to use those which show most dramatically the development of the boy into the great king and saint.

Not only Louis' own life but the century in which he lived was dramatic. His grandfather, Philip Augustus, had pulled the power of the throne out of the mud. The crusades, on the other hand, had introduced a new spirit of brotherhood, for a peasant was the equal of a noble on the distant battlefields of the Holy Land. The nobles, seeing their power dwindle, kept their war horses ready and their war banners flying to remind the king that they had not always been his liege men. It was a hard time for a woman to rule in France. Perhaps none but Louis' mother, Blanche of Castile, could have done it. As a mother she was cold and stern, seldom showing the love she must have felt for her children. As queen regent, ruling for her son until he should come of age, she was the perfect example of justice and strength. All his life, Louis remembered and imitated her ways.

In religion also the thirteenth was a century of dramatic growth. There was the long building of the new cathedrals, notably Notre Dame of Paris, with Gothic arches pointing toward heaven. Dominic had just died, leaving the Rosary to the world. Francis of Assisi had won countless converts to his beautifully simple way of salvation. St. Clare lay helpless in a loft over a chapel in Assisi, mighty in her saintliness.

But there was heresy also. Across the Rhone, in Germany, Frederick II thundered his defiance of the Pope. Frederick had written a book, *The Three Impostors*, of which Jesus was one; yet the holiest places of the Holy Land then lay under his protection. There was need of a saint to be King of France. The time was right for Louis IX, the last crusader.

Perhaps little would be known of Louis as a human being if it were not for the chronicle of John, the Lord of Joinville. John became Louis' friend when both were young. He was among the first to join in the crusade of 1248. For the rest of his life he was the king's confidant. It is pleasant to picture him, a white-bearded old patriarch of ninety or so, sitting in his drafty castle and painstakingly writing down every memory of the man he had known to be a saint. His affection did not keep him from making small criticisms, and as a result Louis the man is as well detailed as Louis the king.

Research into the life and times of a person who lived so long ago is a lengthy process, and I have read and consulted many books. The following, however, have been my main sources of information:

The Good St. Louis and His Times by Bray (London: Griffith and Farran, 1870).

Memoirs of the Crusades by Villehardouin and de Joinville (Number 333 of Everyman's

Library, London and Toronto: J. M. Dent and Sons Ltd., New York by E. P. Dutton, 1908).

The Court of a Saint by Winifred F. Knox (London: Methuen and Company, 1909).

St. Louis and Calvin by M. Guizot (New York: Macmillan and Company, author's note dated 1868).

St. Louis, the Most Christian King by Frederick Perry (New York: G. P. Putnam's Sons, 1901).

CHAPTER ONE

A Crown of Gold for Louis

YOUNG Louis felt very small, standing there among the kneeling nobles. Of all the people jammed into the great cathedral, only one other person was standing—the bishop in gold cope and miter, up before the high altar. He was waiting for Louis to come forward. I can do it, the boy thought. If I keep my eyes on the bishop I can walk to the edge of this platform, go down the steps without stumbling, then up the altar steps. He had practiced it yesterday over and over with his mother and a dozen priests to correct him if he made a mistake. He must make no mistakes now. Anything going wrong might be a bad omen for the years ahead. They had to be good years because they would not belong to him alone. In a few moments now he would be crowned King of France. That was a tremendous thing to be happening to a boy, especially when he was only eleven years old.

His knees began to tremble. He was not afraid, really. But he had fasted and prayed in the church all night, and now it was the middle of the dull November morning, and he was very empty. A few moments ago the Duke of Burgundy had removed the crimson robe Louis had received yesterday when he was knighted, and he wore only the long brown trunk hose and a short white tunic. Without the robe, every one of the hundreds of people in the cathedral could see those trembling knees. He could see them himself, mirrored in the enormous silver ornament fastening the duke's cloak. He could see his own face, too, with the halo of shining yellow hair which hung to his shoulders. The tunic was slit on the shoulders, chest and back for the anointing, and through the slits he felt the chill. He shivered. His mother would be ashamed of him. He should not be thinking of the cold or his emptiness when he was about to become king.

Louis knew he should not turn his head, but at that moment he had to have his mother's approval. Turning his head slowly, he looked up at her, seated on the throne he had just left. Although she was now Queen Regent of France, she was not arrayed in royal robes. She wore pure white in mourning for his father, Louis VIII, who had died so suddenly three weeks before. Her face still showed the marks of her grief, but she was looking down at Louis with stern encouragement, expecting him to go through the long ceremony without a single blunder. His younger brothers, Robert and Philip, never could be counted upon. Kneeling at the foot of the throne, with hands clasped piously, they appeared to be behaving themselves well enough. But Robert, catching Louis' eye, made a face.

The boy who would soon be king almost giggled. Then, with a sick little feeling of fear, his gaze flew back to his mother. God and France, think of nothing but God and France, those had been her final words to him last night. If she had noticed the distraction, she might well order his tutor to whip him, once they had returned to Paris. But the square white frame of her headdress nodded faintly. What a beautiful mother I have, Louis thought, so good to me, so holy. With confidence now, he fastened his attention on the bishop who was a tall golden statue in the candlelight. Straight to the altar the boy walked, and knelt.

Out of the vestry came a long procession of monks and barons headed by the Abbot of St. Remi. The abbot was fat and he wore so many vestments that his hands barely met to hold the sacred vial of oil. The vial was made of glass and inside it the oil looked yellow and thick. It had been borne down from heaven by a dove, so the story went, when the great Clovis had been crowned King of the Franks more than seven hundred years before.

The boy raised his head. The bishop's thumb made cold crosses on his forehead, chest, shoulders, back and elbows. Now he was Louis IX, King of France, ready to be vested in the royal robes. The great emperor Charlemagne had worn them first at his coronation, and after him every king of France for four hundred and fifty years. No wonder the powerful barons of the realm had been quarreling for the past week over who should be chosen to bear the vestments to the altar. It was a great honor even to touch them. Dukes and counts arrayed in the finest of velvet and taffeta and ermine carried the precious things.

"Rise, my lord," the bishop whispered.

Louis got quickly to his feet. The bishop should not have had to remind him.

The robing ceremony was long, with many prayers and much bowing by the barons. Finally they stood back, leaving the boy alone at the foot of the altar. Over the white tunic he now wore a chasuble of bright blue silk, heavily embroidered, and over that the royal mantle of dark red silk lined with ermine. On his feet were blue slippers heeled with golden spurs, around his waist the sheathed sword. His right hand wore the ring and held the scepter, the emblem of his kingly power. In his left was the rod of justice topped by a golden hand. And on his head was the jeweled crown of Charlemagne.

Often last night, while he knelt before the altar, Louis had imagined what this vesting ceremony would be like. Now, wearing the robes, he had but one awful thought: nothing fitted him. He could not loosen his hold even for a second upon the scepter, for then the ring would fall off. And if he could not use his hands, he would step right into the long chasuble which fell to a silken pile before him. The mantle would be no trouble for it was open very wide in front, sweeping back into a train. But the slippers were so large he would most likely walk out of them. And at his first movement the crown would slip down over his ears. Everything had been made for Charlemagne, who must have been a strapping big man. Nobody had remembered that the new king would never fit the vestments.

Anxiously the boy scanned the multitude of faces. Many of the nobles had refused to come to the coronation because they did not want to be ruled by the queen regent, a woman. Would they all be saying now that the king did not fit the throne, either, and set their war banners to flying over their castles the minute they got home?

Six of the peers were approaching to escort Louis back to the throne. Among them was the Duke of Burgundy, dashing and haughty. If he doesn't help me now, Louis thought, then it means he will not be my loyal subject either. There was a hush, as if everyone in the great cathedral sensed that this was a dramatic moment.

The duke paused in front of the new king, taking his time. He had his hair cut very short,

and it was black and curly like the fur lining
his surcoat. He wore so many jewels that they
must have been a weight to carry, and his
eyes glittered like the precious stones. He is
laughing at me, Louis thought in panic. But the
duke bent gracefully, lifted the hem of the
chasuble, and the Count of Bar did the same.

A little murmur ran over the crowd. Louis
smiled, remembered he should be solemn, and
fixed his eyes straight ahead. With all the
confidence in the world, he moved forward. He
had mounted to the throne and was seated before he remembered how worried he had been
that the crown might slide down over his ears.
Nothing had happened to it at all.

Laying aside his miter and staff, the bishop
approached the throne, knelt, and took the oath
of allegiance to the new king. He grunted,
getting up, for he was old and stiff. Louis
noticed uneasily that Robert and Philip, kneeling on the steps, watched the bishop with the
angelic air they always wore when they were
thinking up mischief. They were both in scarlet,
the mourning color of a prince for his father,
but they did not look sad. Robert's cheeks were
as red as his surcoat, and Philip was twisting his
mouth to keep from laughing. Alphonse, the
quiet brother, had grown tired of kneeling and

had seated himself on the step. Isabel, who was only two, sat beside him in her stiffly jeweled little dress and hood, hands folded in her lap and face as grave as the queen regent's.

Approaching the throne now was the papal legate, so dignified that he didn't glance down once to see where he was going. The smallest tug at the carpet could trip him up. Slowly Robert's hand began to slip toward the floor. Louis glanced at his mother. She was not watching.

In desperation, Louis made a small start out of his chair. But Pacifico, his tutor, had stepped quietly out of the crowd and stood with arms folded in sight of the two young princes. Pacifico wore the plain brown robe of St. Francis, and there was a stoutly knotted cord around his waist. He had used that cord upon the young princes, all four of them. Innocently, Robert straightened. Philip suddenly became more angelic than ever. Louis settled back and extended his hand for the legate to kiss.

It was nearly noon when Louis descended from the throne and was finally relieved of the heavy robes of Charlemagne. His mother, who had come into the vestry, stood watching while the attendants put on his first royal attire. The brown hose and white tunic were the same, but now he wore leather shoes, a short red surcoat with the sleeves slit wide and trimmed with ermine, and a red velvet cap with a long point. When the attendants retired, Louis looked at his mother and laughed.

"They fit, Mother. Everything fits!"

The regent had not smiled for the past three weeks. She moved slowly across the stone floor, her long gown making a soft whisper. Her face was almost as white as her headdress. This day must be very difficult for her. Yet through it all she had never looked other than she did now, composed and very beautiful. She was taller than most women, and from her Louis had inherited his blond hair and gray eyes. But even more outstanding than her beauty was the great dignity with which she bore herself, the queenly presence of which the poets wrote.

Blanche laid her hand under the boy's chin and kissed him on the forehead.

"My son, you did very well. You will be a good king."

Louis' heart leaped. Such words of praise from his mother, who never praised her children!

"You have taught me to be good, Mother. You'll teach me to be a king." He touched the stiff serge of her sleeve. Seldom did he feel so close to her. "Mother, you know I didn't sleep last night. I'm tired. Could I take a trencher of bread and meat and go out in the woods with Pacifico . . ."

The regent's straight black brows drew together. "Listen to me, Louis." She spoke very slowly, her voice so low that the prelates and nobles off in the corners could not hear. "You are not merely a royal child any more. You are the king, *you are France!* You do not belong to yourself any more, but to them." The head-dress nodded toward the open door beyond which a throng had gathered.

The boy hung his head. Instantly his mother's hand was under his chin, tilting it up again.

"Do not let them think I am scolding you. I am not. I'm only reminding you of your duty."

"Yes, Mother. God and France."

Her face softened. "That is right, Louis, God first always. I would rather see you lying dead before me than to know you had committed a mortal sin. Be a good man and you cannot help but be a good king."

"Yes, Mother."

"And now we go to the banquet."

"Of course, Mother."

Louis' head was up bravely when he walked beside his mother out into the sunshine. The day had turned warm. The woods would be delightful down by the River Vesle. But this day belonged to the people of Reims and the new king must give it to them. Tomorrow, when the journey home to Paris would begin, he would ride through other towns and that day would belong to those people. All his life would belong to the people, never again to himself.

The people cheered when they saw Louis.

"My liege lord!" they cried, for that meant they were loyal to the king. "God bless you! Long may you reign!"

They stretched out their hands. Some fell on their knees. Several knights in full armor began to push back the crowd.

"Make way for the king!" they shouted. "Way for the king!"

The royal party made slow progress to the bishop's palace where the banquet would be held. At the great entrance the nobles were assembled, a dazzling company in cloth of gold and velvet and ermine. Up against the pillars a hundred or more little page boys waved the brilliant banners of the knights.

But Louis had only glanced at the splendid

assembly. Down below, in the mud, was a handful of beggars. Their hair and beards were matted with straw and dirt, their rags bound on with strings of leather. When they saw the king they began to whine, stretching out their hands like claws.

All the beggars of Reims, Louis knew, were to be fed and given new capes as a mark of royal favor. But these men were different. They had dragged themselves here because they wanted to see the king, not merely to receive alms from the royal treasury.

The knights had halted a few paces off and were looking back at Louis. Blanche waited with cold dignity. But no one was so important to the boy just then as those ten miserable beggars. The Lord had healed ten lepers—and one of these was a leper. Crouching away from the others on the far side of the mud puddle, he kept up his whine.

"Unclean! Unclean!"

Louis knew how this terrible disease had been brought back by crusaders returning from the East and that anyone could be infected by it. That was why the lepers were required to chant their cry of "Unclean!" as a warning to keep people away. Yet, without a thought for his own well-being, the young king ran around the

puddle and bent over the beggar. Then, to the
man's astonishment, he lifted the thin hand and
kissed it.

"I have no purse," he said, "but when the
bread is given out, tell them I asked that you
have two portions."

The beggar, weeping, touched his forehead
to the ground. Over the crowd there ran a
murmur of horror, but through it someone
shouted, "Bravo!" The knights whirled, facing
the throng. Then, as if nothing had happened,
the royal company proceeded up the steps of
the palace and into the banquet hall.

Lying in bed that night, Louis thought he
still could catch the scent of the roast meats and
the herbs with which the food was spiced. The
odor, however, might be only the oil burning
in the clock. The clock was a glass vial with a
spout which held a wick, and as the wick
burned the oil went down, reaching marks on
the glass. The oil had reached the ten o'clock
mark now. Louis should be asleep. Pacifico had
said so nearly an hour ago.

But the boy sat up in the big curtained bed.
The only light in the high tower room was
from the little wick in the clock, and so he
could not see Pacifico. But he could hear him
snoring down on his makeshift bed somewhere

in the shadows. Louis would have liked to talk. He wanted to know what it meant that the Lord had sent ten beggars to him on his coronation day. There was not much of that day left. Two hours until midnight. Was it right to spend those hours lazily in bed?

Carefully, so as not to wake Pacifico, Louis crawled out of the warm covers. Down in the courtyard the troubadours were singing and softly plucking their lutes. He hadn't realized how sleepy he was. The stone floor was cold on his bare feet. Wrapping his night robe tight about him, he padded over to the prie-dieu.

There was just light enough for Louis to see the white figure on the crucifix. He kissed the feet. It would have been nice to climb back into his bed, but a good king would never put comfort before duty.

"Lead me, O Lord, in Thy way and I will walk in Thy truth," he whispered.

He could not remember the rest of it. His head fell on folded arms.

The next thing he knew, Pacifico was lifting him up bodily.

"Put me down!" Louis protested. "I must say my prayers! I must be a good king!"

"Tomorrow you be a good king," Pacifico

grunted. "For today, enough is enough, even of prayers."

And with the boy in his arms he climbed the steps to the bed.

Louis was too sleepy to argue. Pacifico was always right. Curling himself up into a ball, the new King of France went soundly to sleep.

CHAPTER TWO

The Kidnaper's Plot

The February afternoon was rainy and cold. Louis, astride his horse, tried to listen to Pacifico reading the hour of nones. Pacifico's voice was muffled because he held the book under the hooded chape he wore, and with the beat of the rain on Louis' own chape and the rumble of carts and the thump of the horses' feet, it was hard to follow the prayers. This entire journey had been the most uncomfortable he and his mother had made in the year and a half since he had become king. Through two days of winter rain the royal party of a hundred or more had been plodding up from the city of Orleans, stopping at night at some nobleman's castle, moving on in the morning as soon as they had heard Mass. By tomorrow night they would be at home again in Paris.

"Amen," Pacifico intoned.

"Amen," said Louis, and heard the tutor's prayer book slap shut.

The boy twisted around in the saddle. In front of him and behind rode the knights, several hundred of them. A few carried falcons on their wrists; but in the clumsy chape it was hard to tell a knight from a cook's helper. Not far back in the line was the square-topped, heavy carriage in which rode the queen regent. Bringing up the rear, drenched and squeaking, were the big carts carrying the money barrels, the cook with all his equipment, the blacksmith, and the other servants needed to serve so large a company of knights. The queen had intentionally made it a large company. The barons of the kingdom, meeting at Orleans, had to be impressed with the power of the throne. And they had been impressed. All of them, finally, had sworn allegiance to the king.

"I have a wonderful mother," the boy said aloud. "She is a great queen."

Pacifico grunted. "She will have her troubles."

"Oh, not any more, Pacifico! The barons are all our liege men!"

The monk grunted again. "A liege man is a faithful follower. Do you see Peter of Brittany bowing down to a woman ruler?"

"But he took the oath!"

"It was lightly taken."

Louis opened his lips to protest. But there was no denying that grizzled old Peter had been red-faced and angry when he knelt to lay aside his sword and place his hands in those of the king.

"He gave his word, Pacifico! They all did! Even Thibaut of Champagne!"

"Thibaut is not a rebel at heart," said the monk. "He is a poet, a dreamer, and it appeals to him to be ruled by a woman. But not Peter. Not Count Hugh of La Marche. Did the two of them not ride off home even before our party left Orleans?"

Louis answered with another question. "Have you forgotten, Pacifico, that my sister Isabel is to marry Count Hugh's eldest son?"

"Isabel is three years old! She will hardly be married until she is twelve. In nine years, how many times can Count Hugh change his mind?"

Out of patience, the boy spurred his horse into the company of the knights. There was nothing to be gained in arguing with Pacifico. The monk, as well as the whole kingdom of France, would soon see how successful the meeting at Orleans had been.

"Who comes?" a knight called out.

It was not Louis he meant. Over a foggy rise ahead a rider appeared and came galloping toward them. He also wore a waterproof chape, but he had not taken the care to fasten it around him and it flew out like wings. He was dressed in black, and with the black horse and the flapping wings he was like a huge bat looming out of the rain and fog. Even at a distance, Louis recognized him. Only Thibaut of Champagne affected so much black.

"The count brings trouble," Louis heard a knight remark. "Good news is never in such a hurry."

Reining his horse to its haunches before the king, Thibaut wasted no time in greeting.

"Monsieur Louis, we must speak with your mother immediately. Will you come with me to her?"

The company had halted. The knights, without a word, opened an avenue back to the carriage, and the two passed through. Footmen jumped to take the horses, and Louis and the count slid down into the mud. Another footman threw back the heavy curtain which covered the carriage door. Inside, in the gloom, Blanche sat wrapped in a fur-lined cape, her rosary in her hand. Her gray eyes went casually over Thibaut, and she nodded as if it were quite the ordinary thing for one of the most powerful nobles in the realm to come riding breakneck from Paris. Louis felt a thrill of pride. His mother could deal with anything.

The count pushed back his hood. Even soaked as he was, he made it a gallant gesture.

"Madame, I bring news of a plot against the king!"

Blanche's gaze did not waver, but her fingers tightened on the rosary.

"A plot, sir? Who would be plotting against us after taking the oath of allegiance at Orleans?"

"Those who spoke loudest, Madame. Peter of Brittany and Hugh of La Marche."

Louis saw the red color flame into his mother's cheeks.

"What is it they plan, Thibaut?" she asked.

"Nothing less than to kidnap the king, Madame, as he rides back to Paris."

Louis gasped. The color drained from the queen's face. The footman dropped the curtain and had to fumble for it again. The count put one foot on the carriage step, leaning forward to speak earnestly.

"Peter will always be a rebel, Madame Blanche, and Hugh will be ready to follow him. Sooner or later you must fight them to the finish. But our immediate concern is for the safety of the king."

The queen nodded.

"Leave the heavy carts behind," Thibaut said swiftly. "Without them we can travel fast. In a few hours we could reach the strong castle of Montlhery, in sight of Paris."

"But if the enemy is waiting—it will be dark—"

It was not like Blanche to stammer. She is really afraid for me, Louis thought.

"They are not expecting the king until to-morrow. We'll take them by surprise."

For the first time the queen looked at her son. The rosary hung down from her lap and the crucifix trembled. But she gathered it up competently and dropped it into her pocket. She turned to the footman.

"Pierre, tell the master of the grooms to prepare a horse for me. And you, Count Thibaut, will you see to dividing the party? Take every knight with a fast horse, but leave the slow ones behind with the carts. We cannot wait for anyone if we are to reach Montlhery tonight. Go, Pierre!"

She rose as if she would mount her own horse on the instant. The footman, scrambling away, fell into a mud puddle.

Within minutes the king with the queen regent and an escort of knights had left the ponderous carts far behind. The hard riding was exciting. The wind stung and the rain slapped Louis' face. Over hills of soaked brown grass the horses pounded, then down into valleys where peasants' huts were huddled together in fields marked with the stalks of last year's cabbages. Once a hen ran squawking into the road and was trampled under the horses' feet, and a man trudging with a water pail stopped as if he might go to the hen's rescue. Louis would have liked to stop and pay him for the hen, but there was no time. He pulled his hand out from under the chape to wave. The man still stared. He could not know, of course, that this was the king's party desperately riding to escape the kidnapers.

The afternoon deepened into twilight and still the horses raced on. The clouds hung so low that the spiked peaks on the knights' helmets seemed to cut them. With the ground darkening it was impossible to tell whether the water-filled dents in the road were mere puddles or holes deep enough to throw a horse. But there was no time for caution. Somehow the enemy might have received word of this pell-mell flight. Anywhere in the hills they could be lurking. Louis scarcely thought of his own safety. But if the rebels were to seize him, the humiliation would never be lived down by the queen regent. Her power to rule would be broken. The whole future of France might depend upon his safe arrival tonight at Mont-lhery.

It was dark when the party descended into a valley familiar to Louis. He and Robert had come here often to fish in the small stream, only an hour's ride from Paris. Crowning the hills and still visible against the sky were the gnarled oaks where the page boys hunted squirrels. The horses slowed to a trot, filing across the narrow bridge. The king's horse turned aside after crossing the bridge, but immediately Thibaut's hand was on the bridle.

"No, Monsieur Louis!"

"But he's so thirsty!"

"Look on the hilltop!"

Louis glanced up. Against the sky now were forms heavier than the branching oaks—men mounted on horses! They were as still as the trees.

"I fancied this might be the place of ambush," Thibaut said quietly. "In the dark they can't be sure of who we are. Ride on at an even pace, Monsieur Louis. I'll come after you with the queen."

They made a slow ascent out of the valley. Once Louis looked back. The figures remained among the oaks.

"Now *ride!*" Thibaut called when the level plain opened before them.

Every horse sprang to its fullest speed. A few minutes later the great hulking mass of Montlhery loomed out of the night.

The drawbridge was down in place, the gate open, and in the courtyard there were torches flaring in the hands of pages and a huge bonfire for light. Riders streamed in, grooms jumped to take the horses, and talk and excitement ran high.

Being welcomed by the lord and lady of the castle, walking with them into the great hall, Blanche kept her hand on her son's shoulder, an almost unknown gesture of affection. During supper she had him sit beside her and watched him eat although she did not touch the meat that the knight carved before her. Louis knew her concern was not for himself alone, but for France. The king belonged to the people.

With the drawbridge raised and bowmen posted in the towers, the entire company slept safely in the castle that night. By morning the rain had stopped and the sun came up brilliant over the wet plain. Only one thing was amiss. The king was a prisoner in the castle. Out on the plain the knights led by Peter of Brittany and Hugh of La Marche had grown in number to a small army. When a single rider galloped from the gates out on to the road to Paris, he was instantly seized and released only when he was seen to be a groom and not the king.

"There are so many of them!" Louis exclaimed as he stood looking down with Pacifico from one of the turrets. "They'll keep us here like rats in a hole!"

The monk shook his head. "I doubt it. Madame Blanche is more than a match for them."

"Do you know something you're not telling me, Pacifico?"

"Nothing, Monsieur. I am only guessing. But

my guess is that you will be out of here to-day."

"But how, Pacifico? When the groom rode out, they stopped him."

"Yet he must have reached Paris. Look!"

Over the rolling plain the great structure of Notre Dame Cathedral looked like a turtle with raised head. Halfway along the road from the turtle was a gathering of dark specks which soon became people. Others kept flowing up over the rise like ants in orderly fashion. By the end of a half hour the roadsides were lined with people of all ages, old men seated with the children on the grass, younger men walking quietly about, women standing in small groups, all watching the castle.

"I understand now," Louis said at last. "My mother sent a rider to Paris to tell the people of our predicament, and they have come to rescue us."

Pacifico, who had been thoughtfully biting the end of his hood, now pulled the hood up over his head. "Could you have better de-fenders, Monsieur Louis? Come, Madame the Queen must not be kept waiting."

Louis started obediently for the stairs. Again the courtyard was packed with an excited crowd, but now there was gay laughter as the knights swung themselves to their horses. Over in a sunny corner of the wall a troubadour plucked his lute, but only the motion of his hand told of the music. Even the queen regent, bidding good-by to the lord and lady on the steps, appeared to be proudly content. She did not speak to Louis, but she nearly smiled. With the aid of a groom she mounted her horse. Pacifico lifted Louis to his saddle. The draw-bridge came creaking and banging into place, the castle gates were swung wide, and the knights who were in the lead clattered out over the moat, the first one bearing the banner of St. Denis, the oriflamme of France.

There was an audible murmur from the people as the knights rode out. But when they caught sight of the king astride his white horse, his blond hair blowing in the wind and his scarlet tunic aflame in the sun, a cheer started among those near and ran down the long avenue like wind passing over a wheat field. They began the old hymn the crusaders sang when they first caught sight of Jerusalem: "Fair are the meadows, fairer still the woodlands." It was a glorious sound. It seemed to hold back the enemy assembled out on the plain, all armed and mounted.

The queen drew up her horse, and Louis

stopped beside her. He glanced at his mother and smiled. His throat was too tight for speech. When Blanche spoke, her husky voice was even huskier than usual.

"You are France, my son. They love you, but it is not for yourself they do honor, it is for the throne. These are the common people of Paris, the tradesmen and shopkeepers, even the beggars—the heart of France. They have come to defend you. The nobles will try to take power into their own hands, but these people will give it to you. They have done so today. The nobles are powerless against them."

"Yes, Mother," Louis said softly. It was all he could push past the lump in his throat. Along with the hymn there were voices raised in prayer. No enemy could batter down such a bulwark.

Louis had never seen his mother more beautiful than she was this morning in her severe white, her cheeks faintly pink from excitement and her blond hair hanging to her waist under the veil. The shining armor of the knights and their bright banners fluttering around her made a fitting background for such a queen.

"Fifteen months ago, Louis, you were crowned at Reims," she said. "But today—

today, my son, you have become King of France."

Her horse started forward at a walk. Louis followed. Out on the plain the enemy, gathered in harmless knots, folded down their banners and by twos and threes withdrew. As safe as only his people could keep him, the young king passed down the long road and into Paris.

CHAPTER THREE

The Lesson of Belesme

Louis and his brother Robert were tilting at
the quintaine. The winter day was bright and
snappy, the horses were spirited, and each time
a lance struck the quintaine, which was a
wooden man on a pivot, he spun as if he en-
joyed it. This was no time for Pacifico to
stride into the courtyard and beckon sternly to
the young king.

"I must have my turn at the target!" Louis
cried.

He galloped to the starting point and wheeled his horse. Then, lying low, one hand gripping the saddle and the other firmly on the lance, he raced toward the quintaine. The trick was to hit the empty arm and dart away before being struck by the sandbag which was tied to the other arm. Louis was very good at it.

But Robert also had swung his horse. He was in a reckless mood today. With a wild yell he charged at Pacifico. The monk leaped so swiftly out of the way that his bare feet twinkled beneath the robe. Louis struck the quintaine, but he had begun to pull up his horse when he saw his brother's intention and he was slapped soundly by the sandbag.

"Monsieur Robert, I'll get your mother's permission to give you twenty lashes!" Pacifico sputtered.

"You'll have to catch me first!" Robert sang out, and tore away in the direction of the stables where he had been forbidden to go. The day before, he had brought punishment upon himself by liberating ten of the finest falcons.

Louis reined up before Pacifico. The tutor was used to being teased by the young princes. He jerked the cord tighter about his waist and spoke sharply.

"Monsieur Louis, Madame the Queen desires you to wait upon her at Poissy. Immediately!"

"Is it Count Peter again, Pacifico?"

The monk gave a shrug that loosened the cord. "The messenger did not say. But a year has passed since he plotted to kidnap you. It is time for him to be growing restless."

Louis could not help a longing glance at the painted face of the quintaine. He had visited his mother this morning. Why did she have to summon him again?

He rode unattended out to the castle where he had been born and where his mother had lived since the death of Louis VIII. Giving his horse to a groom, he went straight to the high, drafty chamber where the regent held her conferences. The Bishop of Paris, who because of his wisdom and age was a trusted adviser, sat on the dais beside Blanche. At Louis' entrance they both looked up as if they had been talking earnestly. In the great, dark room candles had been lighted, and the bishop's heavily embroidered robes were rich beside the queen's black. Her headdress was a plain black hood and she wore no jewels. Any other woman would have been ugly in such attire, but Blanche was beautiful. She descended from the dais, her long gown falling in a train on the steps.

"Yes, Madame," said Louis.

"My son, Count Peter has taken up arms against us," she said abruptly.

He was not surprised at the news. For months Peter had been acting like a spoiled child, laying waste his own lands to draw attention to his peevishness. The regent had sent him a protest which he had ignored. No one had expected that Peter would suddenly behave himself. Why, then, was the queen so upset she appeared to be almost ill?

"Count Hugh of La Marche is Peter's ally," she added.

Louis smiled. "Hugh and Peter together are not equal to us, Madame! We'll set them spinning like a pair of quintaines!"

But the old bishop raised his white head and looked down at Louis with a falcon's keenness. "The King of England is with them, Sire."

The boy's smile died. War between England and France! With Peter and Hugh to burrow through the kingdom after all the nobles who still resented being ruled by a woman, such an army could be raised that no hastily summoned force could stop it. No wonder the queen's face was white and set.

"Madame," Louis said, "Henry of England has made a truce with us. He has agreed to peace."

"Peter has helped him forget it. Normandy once belonged to England. Peter has promised it back to Henry in return for aid against us."

"Peter will have to conquer Normandy before he can give it to Henry!"

"And he has not conquered Normandy yet," the bishop said, gently pounding the sore knee that gave him a limp when he walked. "There is nothing to be gained by admitting defeat before it comes. Gather your knights, Madame, send them out under Archibald of Bourbon. He is as loyal as your own son."

Blanche turned to him, and she seemed to grow taller as she spoke. "Send them, my lord? I shall lead them myself!"

The bishop's hand paused. "It is winter in the North. There is cold and snow to test the endurance of men! It is no place for a woman!"

"We shall not discuss it further, William." The queen turned to Louis. He wanted to throw his arms around her and tell her how proud he was of her courage.

But all he said was, "Madame, you will permit me to go with you?"

"You are the king, are you not?"

Out of the corner of his eye, Louis saw that the bishop made a gesture as if he washed his hands of the whole affair.

"I have summoned the nobles," Blanche said. "As soon as they can call their knights together, we leave for the North." Her gray eyes narrowed. "It pleases me that your first thought was to go with the army. You will make a good king, my son."

She nodded in dismissal. Louis walked along the strip of red carpet to the curtained doorway, but with his hand ready to draw back the curtain, he stopped.

"Mother."

The queen, at the foot of the dais, turned. Louis had not called her Mother for a long time.

"Mother, I must confess that when Pacifico came with your message, I didn't want to leave our game."

Blanche waited coldly. He swallowed and continued. "I was with Robert. We were tilting at the quintaine." Again he paused, but there was no word from her. "I'm sorry, Madame," he said. Raising the curtain, he departed.

Slowly he walked through the hall, his feet whispering in the straw which covered the floors in winter. Perhaps, he thought, it would have been better not to mention his reluctance to leave the game. His mother was always fair but never sympathetic. She did not approve of such sports as tilting and falconry, even though she permitted her sons to indulge in them. To allow interest in a game to compete with his duty as king—wasn't that sinful?

"Wait, my son," said a quiet voice behind him.

It was the bishop, slightly out of breath from hurrying, leaning hard on his stick. He regarded the boy affectionately.

"You have a tender conscience, Monsieur Louis. It must not be a torture to you."

"But I should think first of our people! I am the king!"

"God's own Son was a King, also, but He was first a Boy. He does not expect you to be everything at one time. You are a boy of fourteen."

Louis could make no reply. If only his mother could give him such understanding!

The bishop, seeming even to understand his silence, linked his arm in the young king's. "I am pleased that you are going with the army. The nobles will rally to your banner. It will be such an army as never was seen in France!"

Ten days later, on the cold northern plain,

Louis remembered the bishop's prophecy. It had indeed come true. Gathered before him was such an army as never had been seen in France —a company of some seventy men. Instead of the numbers which might be expected to rally to the king's banner, the nobles had come with only two knights apiece, an insult to the queen. With the Duke of Burgundy as their spokesman, they sat their horses in comparative comfort with their backs to the wind while Louis and his mother were forced to face the biting gale. The duke was not even wearing armor. He regarded the queen with daring impudence.

"I asked for an army!" Blanche said shortly when the duke did not speak. "Where is it?"

"You asked for all available knights. We regret, Madame, that so few were ready."

"Peter and Hugh are ready!"

"We regret that also, Madame. But in view of the fact that our forces are so small, and unarmed, we feel that the only possible course for us is to return home. We could not sacrifice our men in so uncertain a cause."

Louis could hardly keep silent. The cause was not uncertain! Let the queen retire from the field with the laughter of these powerful barons to follow her, and Peter and Hugh would be the rulers of France!

The wind was flapping Louis' chape so loudly that he had not heard the approach of other horsemen until a groom called out. Over the bleak plain an army was thundering, helmeted and armed in battle array.

"Peter!" Louis gasped, and a great chill of fear prickled down his spine.

But in the next second he knew that this was not Peter's army. Out ahead, galloping across the scattered patches of snow, was a rider dressed in black and mounted on a coal black horse.

"Thibaut of Champagne!" someone exclaimed. "Does he come as friend or enemy?"

It could be either, Louis knew. Several times during the past year the count had made complaints to the queen, but he had never seemed to be very much in earnest about them. Pulling his horse to its haunches, his black eyes scanned the company.

"I see, Madame Blanche, how your loyal nobles have rallied to your banner!" he spat out. "Look at the men I have brought for you! From Champagne and Brie and Chartres, three hundred knights and all their liege men! Now let the squalid men of Burgundy return home if they will! We shall defeat Peter without them!"

Pulling his sword from the scabbard, the count waved it dramatically. The duke's face flushed dark red. His henchmen hung their heads.

But from Thibaut's army came a cheer, banners were lifted high. The seventy knights of Burgundy who had sat so dispiritedly now joined the others, and there were more cheers.

"We have won, Madame!" Louis cried.

"Not yet. We must make careful plans," the queen said, but her relief was easily seen.

His mother was too cautious, Louis thought several times that afternoon. In the great hall of the castle in which they had spent the night, the queen and her officers shaped out an attack while Louis listened. A map was spread out on the table. Under the table the dogs still gnawed at bones thrown them during the noon meal. And the Master of the Bowmen gnawed at small details as monotonously as the dogs. He was going over his line of march for the sixth time when a messenger interrupted. Count Peter, the herald said, had lost courage and shut himself up in the castle of Belesme. Henry of England had put off joining the French until they could present him with at least one victory.

"See!" Thibaut exulted. "Already Peter has admitted defeat!"

The Master of the Bowmen disagreed. He was an enormous man, and he blew through his beard when he talked.

"Peter has merely retired, Count Thibaut. He has admitted nothing. The moment our army disperses, he will begin his plundering again."

The queen's eyes glittered. "We shall attack Belesme!"

Everyone was silent, staring at her.

"But—but, Madame!" the master sputtered.

"Perhaps Madame does not recall the situation of the castle," Thibaut said gently as if he were explaining to a child. "It is a natural fortress. Many times its walls have been stormed without success. It is impregnable."

"Nothing is impregnable. We attack at dawn."

The queen looked around the startled company, and again Louis felt such a surge of pride that it drowned out any misgivings.

"I shall lead the army myself!" she declared.

She appeared not to hear the gasp that swept the company. No one dared argue with her.

At dawn she was on the plain before Belesme with the army.

The cold was so intense that the vapor froze on the horses' nostrils, and the edge of a helmet was like thin ice where it touched a cheek; but the queen and the young king, armored like the rest, sat their horses only a few hundred yards back from the castle of Belesme. Its moat was wide, reflecting the gray sky in muddy water. The walls were solid stone. No banner flew from the round tower of the keep. No bowmen appeared on the wall above the drawbridge nor anywhere in the turrets.

"So Peter is hiding," Thibaut said contemptuously. "Very well, let us draw him out!"

Leaving Louis and his mother, he spurred his horse ahead.

A few minutes later the army lunged forward. A hail of arrows hit the wall. Up in the turrets, Peter's bowmen suddenly came to life and sent back an answering storm. There was confusion among the queen's forces and they began to withdraw.

"We will take Belesme!" Blanche said grimly.

But a second storming in the late afternoon was no more successful. When night fell over the snowy plain, the cold seemed more intense. Louis rode through the scattered ranks and heard discontented murmurings. With the coming of darkness many knights would desert. And who could blame them?

The boy returned to the campfire. The fire was skimpy. There were no fires at all anywhere else.

"We have no choice but to withdraw," Thibaut was saying. "We cannot ask the men to stay here cold and hungry."

"You brought food for your men, did you not?" Blanche demanded.

"Yes, Madame. But there are no fires to cook it."

"Then there will be fires! Marshal, get me twenty men and carts! Immediately!"

"But Madame—"

"I too am hungry! The peasants have their winter's supply of wood in their dooryards. We shall buy it from them at so good a price they will be glad to sell. Bring up the money carts! Come, Louis! And you, Thibaut, spread the word that help is coming!"

Riding with his mother through the countryside, coming back to see her move among the tents, encouraging the men, Louis knew that this was the kind of leader he must be for the people of France. Not only was she a fine diplomat but also a military leader. It was she alone who held the army together through that bitter night, she alone who must be credited with the victory.

For it was a victory. The next day, Belesme fell.

Louis, watching from a distance with the queen as the great gates were battered down, could imagine Peter cringing inside, perhaps already kneeling with his sword laid before him on the cobblestones.

"What will be their punishment, Madame?" the boy asked.

"How would you deal with them, my son?"

"I should spare their lives."

"Because you pity them?"

"Yes, Madame."

"Justice must never be swayed by pity. At times you must exercise your right of death as well as life over your people. We shall spare Peter and Hugh not for their own sake but because we must rule through them. We need them. And I believe—" The queen paused, for the gate was going down with a fearsome rending of timbers. "I believe our malcontents have learned that the power lies in the throne. That is the lesson of Belesme."

"Yes, Madame," said Louis.

But for him the lesson was a little more. His

mother had added to the pattern which he must follow as king. In courage and resourcefulness as well as piety and statesmanship, she would always be his example.

CHAPTER FOUR

A Bride for the King

Louis had spent a long afternoon working
with the monks at Royaumont. Six years before, when he was only thirteen, he and his
mother had founded the abbey. At first, as a
penance, he had come several times a week to
work at the stonecutting beside the silent monks.
A little later Robert had come with him. But
during the past year he had been finding less
and less time for the stonecutting. And Robert
never came any more.

Pausing at the edge of the clearing, Louis

looked back at the place he had left. The chapel was completed now. He had just heard vespers in it with the monks. Over the great piles of white stone where the cutters had worked the dust was settled. He ought to come again tomorrow—but there would be a falcon hunt. He might have asked permission tonight for a short visit with Pacifico, who had retired here to follow the rule of Francis—but a new minstrel would be singing in the courtyard, and a band of jugglers might happen to stop by. And he would have to change his clothes. The bright green taffeta surcoat was white with dust and his long hose soiled.

Turning into the woods path, Louis walked swiftly toward the place where he had left his horse. From up ahead, in the clearing around the refectory, came the quiet rumble of men's voices. The neighboring peasants gathered here every evening for an hour of recreation. Each man passed his tankard through the refectory door to the monk and received it back filled with wine. The small coppers added to the income of the monastery, and the peasants drank sedately and exchanged news. For most of them it was the only means of learning what was going on in the kingdom. Sometimes Louis stopped to chat with them. Not tonight. The daughter of the Black Princess of Lorraine would be with her mother among the company to hear the minstrel. She was his own age, nineteen—

Louis stopped short on the path. From the other side of the thicket a gruff voice had spoken the name of the Black Princess' daughter.

"She is not the one to be Queen of France! No, the old queen would never stand for it!" the voice ended.

"Louis has no thought of making her his wife," a second voice said. "He likes to dance with her, nothing more."

"My son is a page at the palace," a third came in over the others, "and he says young Louis does not spend the time in the chapel that he used to spend."

"He will be a good king!" the first speaker said with heat. "His mother has made him godly! He knows the meaning of justice!"

"Oh, a good enough king, but no saint," said another voice. "He likes pleasure. Hasn't he hunted lions in Caesarea with a bow and arrow?"

"And brought them down, too!" said the father of the page. "Don't we want our king to live like a king, wear fine clothes, go to the hunt with the best falcons?"

"Our children could eat for a day on what it takes to feed a falcon!"

Louis waited to hear no more. Walking quietly back up the path, he came again, whistling. This time, as he passed, the voices were discussing the cabbage crop.

When he reached the palace he went straight to the chapel and knelt before the altar. Never in his life had he been so strangely frightened. The pleasures he had indulged in with his brothers were only the usual diversions for young men of noble rank. His clothes were not extravagant for a nobleman. But he was not a baron. He was a king, and he must be a good one. It was not enough that he give alms generously to the poor and found churches and abbeys. He always attended carefully to the business of the kingdom under his mother's direction, but every king must do that. For him there was something more. His mother was right in her disapproval of the hunting and dancing. Nothing must come between him and his devotion to France.

When the morning made bright pictures once again of the windows, and the household filed in for Mass, Louis still knelt before the altar.

After Mass, he rode to Poissy and went straight to the chamber where he always had his conferences with his mother. She was there before him, seated in a high-backed chair with papers spread on the table in front of her. William, Bishop of Paris, was with her. Something of importance must be afoot.

Louis would have liked to speak with his mother alone. He bowed a good morning. Blanche gave him a searching look.

"You are pale this morning, my son. Are you ill?"

"No, Madame. I spent the night in the chapel."

The faintest smile touched the queen's lips. The bishop nodded at his gnarled hands.

"We have arranged for you to marry," Blanche said so shortly that it seemed she was testing the effect of the announcement upon her son.

Louis bowed again, hoping it would hide his sudden flush. He had come this morning to ask his mother to find him a wife. How was it that she could always anticipate his needs so accurately?

"William has just returned from making the

agreements," the queen went on. "The girl is
Marguerite, daughter of Count Raymond of
Provence. She has been well brought up. She is
fourteen years of age. She will make a most
suitable wife."

"And queen," said the bishop. "Some day
she will be Queen of France."

The regent frowned. She would not care to
have a girl of fourteen replace her on the
throne.

Disregarding the bishop, she continued, "You
must ask formally for Marguerite's hand, although the arrangements are made. And you
may choose a date yourself."

"Make it soon, Louis," the bishop added.

So William too had heard of Louis' interest
in the daughter of the Black Princess.

There was a long discussion of the dowry
to be paid by Count Raymond, who was well
known to be poor. The young king was not
concerned. The first understanding he must
have with his new wife would be in regard
to the routine of their daily lives. There would
be no hunting, no dancing, no minstrelsy.
Marguerite must help him to be a good king.

The arrangements were quickly made with
Count Raymond of Provence, who was not
worried about the size of the dowry since he

had no intention of paying it. On the twenty-seventh of May, 1234, Louis and Marguerite would be married. Three weeks before, a glittering company of knights and bishops and noblemen was dispatched to Provence to escort Marguerite to Sens. The entire kingdom was in a state of celebration. Alms were given in every village and city, Masses were sung for the young couple in every church on the wedding day.

And in the massive Cathedral of Sens, Louis saw his bride for the first time.

She came to the altar holding her father's arm, a small, dark-eyed, pretty girl, pale and nervous. Her cloth of gold dress was so heavy that she walked with small jerky steps even though several young girls held up the train. Her dark hair was held back in a jeweled snood, and over it she wore a white veil embroidered with tiny stars. A few curls had escaped around her face, giving her the look of a little girl who had just run in from play. She gave one frightened glance at the tall, handsome, fair-haired knight who would be her husband and her hands, tight together, stopped their trembling. Louis was as splendid as anyone could wish in long blue hose, a blue satin tunic and a red velvet surcoat lined with ermine.

A king must be finely arrayed for his wedding.

The ceremony was long, and after it the festivities stretched into the night. Louis, alone in the chapel of the castle where he was lodged with his attendants, heard the minstrels singing until dawn. On that morning, Marguerite was crowned Queen of France. For three days the royal party remained in Sens, and there was merrymaking by the entire city. Louis appeared in public with his bride, but he took part in none of the amusements, and through the three nights he knelt in prayer in the chapel. Until they went aboard the barge for the journey down the river to Paris, he had not seen his wife except at the public ceremonies.

But now they were out on the river, seated together under a canopy on the barge. There were boatmen and ladies-in-waiting, and people over on the banks, but the queen regent had a barge to herself and for the first time Louis and Marguerite were comparatively alone.

This was the opportunity the young king had been waiting for, and now he did not quite know how to begin. He had many things to explain to his wife about life in the palace, yet he did not want to make the prospect austere or forbidding. He was searching for words when he heard her laugh.

"Look, Louis! Look at the goat!"

He followed her pointing finger. A peasant family stood on the bank, staring solemnly. They had even brought their animals to see the king and queen pass by. A boy held a cat, the man had a cow on a tether, the grandmother stood with her arm across a goat's back. The cow had flowers on her horns. The goat wore a collar of flowers and he was eating away everything he could reach.

Louis, laughing, waved and the entire family waved back. When he turned to Marguerite, he was surprised to see that she was not even smiling now.

"Is something the matter, my dear?" he asked gently.

She swallowed hard before she answered. "We had beautiful goats in Provence."

So that was it. She was lonesome. She never had been away from her mother and sisters. And Louis knew his own mother would never show her any affection. He and Marguerite must build a life that would more than take the place of the warm, fun-loving household she had left. Only it would be different. Very different.

"Marguerite," he began, "I believe you and I will be happy together. We will be happier, however, if you understand the kind of life we must lead."

"Oh, I do understand!" she said quickly. She was dressed in pink and white, and her hair hung loose in curls around her shoulders. She looked even younger than her fourteen years. "Mama explained what it means to be Queen of France."

Louis, fighting down the uneasiness that suddenly beset him, wondered whether the Bishop of Paris would be surprised that already the problem had arisen.

"My mother is Queen of France," he said. "But you are the king's wife. Your aim above all must be like mine, to make me a good king."

Marguerite nodded, but a little uncertainly. Perhaps Mama had not covered this point.

"God and France will always come first," Louis went on. "We must give all the time we can directly to God, hearing Mass and the canonical hours and saying our prayers. But our whole lives, no matter what we are doing, must be dedicated to Him."

"Oh, of course!" Marguerite murmured, but almost too readily.

She does not understand, Louis thought sadly. But he continued, "We are going to live in as plain a fashion as Christ did when He was on earth. When we return to Paris the falcons will be liberated because there will be no more hunting. In dress, we shall wear simple things except for state functions. For those, we will dress as befits royalty. Our eating will be very plain. I would like to fast every Friday on bread and water—"

He stopped, thinking that this long list of rules might frighten Marguerite. But to his delight, she answered quickly.

"Mama explained that a good wife must always obey her husband. If these are your wishes, they are also mine."

Louis drew a long breath of relief. He had not realized the depth of his own anxiety. Marguerite had been brought up in a court where every lady had her own troubadour to sing songs and write poetry to her, perhaps finally to go off on crusade to sing his songs to the Blessed Virgin in the Holy Land. For the new little queen, there would be no troubadours. There would be, instead, the cold eye of the regent to watch her every move.

"But we will be happy together!" Louis said aloud, almost defiantly. "In following my way, we will find holiness!"

On their first morning in Paris, Louis began to lead Marguerite along his way of holiness.

It was only a little after dawn when they slipped out of the palace and into the street that wound to Notre Dame Cathedral. The church and the palace, as well as shops and houses of tradespeople, were crowded onto this small Island of the City, with the Seine River dividing to go around it. Where the river became a single stream again below the island, stood the old prison fortress, the Louvre, built by Louis' grandfather, Philip Augustus. Philip, infuriated by the stench and the uproar caused by carts getting stuck in the mud, had seen to it that the streets were paved with cobblestones, and he had built a wonderfully beautiful white wall to enclose his city. But he had not been able to root out the squalor. Around the cathedral, in the very shadows of its flying buttresses, were hovels occupied by jongleurs, robbers and cutthroats.

At this hour the city was as quiet as it ever could be. The beggars had crawled into whatever holes they could find, and the university students were asleep on the straw scattered for them over around the Hill of St. Genevieve. A little later the hawkers would crowd into the square before Notre Dame to sell their apples and cheese, hot bread and herring. But now it was quiet, and the young royal couple hurried up the steps and into the cathedral.

Together they knelt through the Mass and for a long thanksgiving afterward. Louis already had heard matins shortly after midnight in the palace chapel, yet he showed no sign of fatigue. He pretended not to see how Marguerite was hiding yawns. Finally he rose from his knees.

"You may wait here for me if you wish," he whispered.

The girl shook her head. Louis smiled happily. He was very much pleased with his wife.

In the vestry a beggar was waiting, filthy and old and somewhat embarrassed. An acolyte stood with a basin of water and a towel. The beggar was seated on a stool. Louis took the towel and fastened it about his waist. Then, kneeling, he lifted one of the old man's horny feet into the basin. He washed carefully and well. This was something our Lord had done with humility and patience, a symbol of the washing away of sin. Louis forgot that the others might not find it so beautiful until he looked up and saw Marguerite standing with eyes averted and the beggar very red in the face. Rising, he laid his hand on the old man's shoulder.

"Thank you, my friend," he said. "Without you to lend me your poor body, I could not perform this blessed work of charity. So you have gained spiritually as much as I."

He opened the crusader's purse hanging from a strap over his shoulder, but suddenly thinking better of it he took the whole purse and thrust it into the beggar's hands.

"Take it," he said, "and when you have spent the money, come to the palace and my almoner will give you more."

Muttering his thanks, the beggar stumbled out of the vestry. Louis turned to Marguerite and took her hands in his.

"You will get used to it, my dear. Every Friday we will perform this work of charity. You will come to love it as much as I do."

"Yes, Louis," the girl said softly. It reminded him of the way he used to reply to his mother.

He squeezed her fingers tightly. One of them wore the wedding ring. Inside the ring was the inscription he had caused to be put there. He must never forget it, because they would be the three loves of his life: "God, France, and Marguerite."

CHAPTER FIVE

The King Is a General

THE banquet which took place at Saumur on a summer day in 1241 would be talked about for years after. Louis intended it to be so. His brother Alphonse had just been knighted and made Count of Poitiers, and the full court was assembled to do him honor. The pomp and ceremony also reminded the barons of the power of the throne. The hall had been built in the form of a cloister, with a covered walk enclosing a large court. Out in the court, which was open to the sky, the greater number of guests were seated, their scarlet and cloth of gold brilliant in the August sun. Within the walk, which opened on the court in continuous lofty arches, the royal tables had been set.

At the king's table were noblemen of the highest rank, among them Count Peter of Brittany and Count Hugh of La Marche, and Count Thibaut of Champagne wearing a gold cap the like of which had never been seen in France. Before each of the seated guests a nobleman served the meat, with Robert serving before Louis. Three barons stood behind the table as a guard of honor, and behind them were thirty of their knights in silk tunics, and then such a number of sergeants wearing the coat of arms of the new count that they were an army in themselves.

Louis was well pleased. Today he was clothed as a king should be, in a tunic of blue satin and surcoat and mantle of samite lined with ermine. He had eaten well, also, because it was not seemly for the host to eat lightly at a banquet. Only one regret nagged at him. Marguerite was not present. Queen Blanche, now presiding over her own table at the farther end of the walk, had found so many reasons why the young queen should not attend that at last even Louis had given in. For seven years

Marguerite had been his wife and their daughter Blanche was now a year old, but the queen mother had not accepted the fact that a younger woman occupied the throne.

"You frown, Louis," said Robert. "Does something not taste right?"

Louis shook his head. For some time an extremely handsome young knight had been standing against an arch near the table, his eyes following the king's every motion. Now, to turn aside Robert's attention, Louis indicated the young man.

"Ask him to sit with us."

Robert delivered the invitation and the young knight responded eagerly. His hair was dark and hung straight to his shoulders, his features were strong. On his mantle was embroidered a coat of arms.

"You are of the family of Joinville," Louis said. "Simon is my liege man."

"I am John, Sire, his eldest son."

"Sit with me, John of Joinville."

The noblemen moved, some distastefully. They did not approve of the king's way of inviting strangers to his table, but at least this knight was better than the beggars who always shared the meat at Louis' table at home.

The king paid no attention to his guests' displeasure. Something about this young man drew him completely. Perhaps it was a promise of frankness, as if he would speak truth without hesitation.

"What do you know of me, John?" Louis asked.

The knight answered instantly. "In 1239, you sent a crusade to the Holy Land. You were bitterly disappointed when they returned after only a year."

Louis laid down the bit of peacock meat he had taken in his fingers. "Why was I disappointed?"

"Because they had gone in your place, Sire. You felt that their defeat was yours."

"How old are you, John?"

"Sixteen, Sire."

"Ten years younger than I, and yet you speak to me like a father!"

John did not join in the laughter. He looked instead as if the king had rebuked him. Louis leaned toward him, speaking so the others could not hear.

"The return of the crusade after so short a time was disappointing to me, but I was not surprised at its lack of success. Thibaut of Champagne, the leader, wrote songs to the

Blessed Mother instead of sending arrows into her enemies."

The young knight looked full at Louis, his dark eyes shining. "Sire, you know as I do that no crusade will be successful until you lead it yourself!"

Louis' heart seemed to leap into his throat. The idea of crusading was his cherished dream, but a secret one.

"When you go, Sire, I'll be with you!" John declared, and in spite of the fact that he was at a banquet table, he sank to his knees before the king.

Louis laid his hand on the young man's shoulder and felt it tremble.

"John," he said solemnly, "I promise you that as soon as France can spare me, I'll go on crusade. And you will be my liege man!"

Through the rest of the banquet the barons all joined in the talk, but Louis was quiet. John had stirred his dream. Five years before, in 1236, Blanche had ended her regency and handed over to Louis a kingdom well united under the crown. By this full court in his former domain, the King of England would be shown that any power he ever had held in France was at an end. Even Peter and Hugh, here at the table, were again accepted into the inner circle of the king's friends. How could anyone, even the queen mother, insist that France still needed her ruler at home? Now he could go, Louis thought, now he could see the Holy Land. Tomorrow the royal company would proceed to Poitiers, where Alphonse would be invested with the reins of government. Then the way for crusade would be open!

The ceremonies at Poitiers seemed long to Louis. All the vassals were in attendance. Count Hugh and his wife, Isabelle, were received by Louis and the queen mother in a private chamber, a favor befitting their high rank. For Hugh's wife was the widow of the late King John of England and the mother of the present king, Henry III. All was done carefully according to custom.

Yet a note from an unnamed informer awaited Queen Blanche upon her return to Paris. The Countess Isabelle, the note said, had been highly insulted because she had not been invited to sit beside the queen mother during the audience but had been forced to stand like any common vassal. Hugh, the note added, was so incensed at this treatment of his wife that he would not pay homage to Count Alphonse, who himself was only a vassal of the king, but would hold his lands as an English possession and pay homage to Henry III.

Louis was sick at heart. Not only did this mean war, no doubt with England to back up Hugh, but it meant also the postponement of his secret dream of crusade. He could only proceed, however, as if he knew nothing of Hugh's intentions. In the late fall of the same year, 1241, he instructed Alphonse to hold his first court in Poitiers.

It was John of Joinville who brought the king news of the disruption of the court. He had ridden hard up from Poitiers, outdistancing the regular messengers, but he refused food or rest.

"I must tell you what has happened, Sire!" he begged.

"Nothing good, John?" Louis asked.

The young man jerked his sword from the scabbard and threw it to the floor.

"That is what I would like to show Hugh, the naked sword! When you go into battle, Sire, I'll be beside you!"

Louis pushed aside the rolled parchments he had been reading and sat on the edge of the table.

"Tell me, John. Did Alphonse not make the

proper arrangements for the count's entertainment?"

"Proper, Sire? You yourself would have had no better! The finest tents I have seen!"

"And Hugh was not satisfied?"

"He burned them, Sire!"

"*Burned* them?"

"To the ground! He came on a war horse with his wife on the pillion behind him, and he had a troop of men-at-arms also mounted on war horses and carrying their crossbows in their hands! They were ready for battle!"

The king was silent for a long time.

"These lands of Aquitaine were conquered by the brave King Clovis and have been fiefs of the throne for seven hundred years," he said at last. "Now Hugh denies his allegiance. In fact, he shows open rebellion. What would you do, John?"

The young knight pointed to his naked sword which still lay on the floor. Louis nodded. Not even Robert pleased him as much as this John of Joinville, for Robert was impetuous and flighty. John, although just as daring, showed a maturity far beyond his years.

"John, between king and subjects there must be understanding. If I were to say to Hugh, very well, go and be the vassal of the English king, I would be saying also to the people of the province that they must pay homage to a foreign king. And that would be unjust. They are Frenchmen. I am their monarch." He turned away, picked up a parchment and threw it down. "And all this has come about because my mother did not invite Hugh's wife to be seated in our presence!"

"The heap was already piled for the burning, my lord," said John. "This incident was only the spark to set it afire."

John was right. Within a few weeks Hugh and his army took to plundering the lands belonging to the throne. Word came to the palace that Hugh's allies were tardy in coming to his aid; that his stepson, Henry of England, kept giving excuses; that Raimond, Count of Toulouse, was openly trying to sidestep the trouble.

Louis did not wait for the enemy to gather forces. With four thousand knights and twenty thousand men-at-arms, he marched down into the south of France. All along the way other forces joined him until there was no numbering the army. Strong fortresses fell with almost no resistance.

"It is no war at all!" Robert complained to Louis and young John of Joinville one evening as they awaited their evening meal in front of the king's tent. The tents of the army lay like toadstools to the horizon with banners fluttering and the oriflamme of France streaming out above them all.

"Our friend Hugh of La Marche has lost heart," said John.

Louis was about to reply when there was a disturbance at the side of the tent. Two ruffians in torn tunics came scrambling across the grass and threw themselves at the king's feet. Robert and John sprang up. But the guards were before them. Falling upon the two strangers, they dragged them away from the king. A marshal pounded around the tent, followed by a cook's helper.

"What is all this?" Louis demanded. "Who are these men?"

"Poisoners, Sire!" the marshal panted. "We caught them in the very act of putting poison into the food which the cook is preparing for you!"

The men fell to their knees, lamenting loudly.

"Mercy, master, mercy!"

"Why should I show mercy?" Louis demanded. "Did you not know what you were doing?"

"We knew! But we were only carrying out the orders of the Countess Isabelle!"

The king was stunned. He had not dreamed that a subject of his would resort to such trickery.

"Take them away, Marshal," he ordered. "Take them away—and hang them!"

The wretches clutched the ground, but the guards jerked them up and pushed them along down the hill where they disappeared among the tents.

"It is not out of vengeance that I have ordered them hanged," Louis said in a trembling voice. "For my own body I do not care. But the nobles who should be my loyal vassals have plotted too long against me! For the good of France they must be shown that no power can shake the throne!"

Entering his tent, he paused. "I bid you to fast with me until morning and pray for the souls of those two poor sinners," he said to the awe-struck company.

He knelt that night in prayer until he fainted from fatigue.

In the morning a messenger bearing a white banner came into the camp. He bore a scroll from Henry of England. Henry had just landed at Royen at the mouth of the Gironde River, only a few miles away. He regarded the truce between France and England now at an end, since he must defend his stepfather's rights.

Louis made a quick reply. "Tell your lord that I have not broken the truce. I do not make war with England. I do, however, claim the right to punish a rebellious vassal, which Hugh is. If your king chooses to fight by the side of Hugh, then that is his own affair. My men will make ready for the field!"

At the head of his army, Louis rode toward the mouth of the Gironde River. Before the Castle of Taillebourg they met the enemy under the command of Hugh and Henry. Across the small Charente River was the town of Saintes, and the only passage was a narrow stone bridge. Louis, without a thought for his personal safety, charged with his knights onto the bridge. The English met them there and broadswords and lances flashed in the sun. On either side of the bridge the water was flailed by the king's men-at-arms swimming in their heavy armor. The battle was waged so fiercely by the French that the English fell back, but only to get their breath. A second wave rushed forward, to be beaten back again. This time the enemy appeared to be routed. There were losses on both sides. Alphonse had been wounded, although not seriously; and the son of the Count of La Marche was taken prisoner.

Louis, well pleased with the day, made camp around the castle of Taillebourg. A few of the knights slipped over into the town of Saintes where the English had taken refuge and came back with the report that Henry and Hugh were having a violent quarrel.

"Why should they quarrel?" Louis asked.

"Because, my lord," said an older knight, "Henry has found out that this trouble was all the doing of his mother the Countess Isabelle. She wrote letters to him, signing the name of Count Hugh, and told him that if he would furnish the money then Hugh would furnish the men and Henry would get back Aquitaine as his prize of war."

"Henry's army is deserting," said another knight. "They wish to travel home to England through France. We can easily catch the dogs!"

"Hugh is in a panic because he has lost his son," said the first knight. "That is too big a price to pay for the countess' whim."

Louis listened to all of this quietly.

"Hugh has not lost his son," he said. "Why should I take the boy's life simply because he fell prisoner to us?"

"But your brother Alphonse was wounded,

my lord!" a knight protested. "Surely Hugh should pay!"

"He will pay, but not with his son's life. Why should I exact the supreme penalty from a boy who only obeyed his father in going into battle against us?"

The knights could not reply. One at a time, they moved away. Only Joinville was left before the tent.

Louis turned to him, smiling. "John, we have won a great victory. France is finally a kingdom."

"It means more, Sire," John said in his quiet way. "You have shown yourself to be a fine general, as capable as your own mother when she held the army together before Belesme. It was folly for you to fight on the bridge today, but your men followed you, and won. They will follow you anywhere!"

"To the Holy Land, John?" the king asked softly.

"Yes, my lord! You and France are ready for crusade!"

For a long time, Louis was silent. Looking out over the city of tents with the banners again flying and the oriflamme high over all, he saw that city not on the soggy river bottom of Taillebourg but on the wide slopes leading up to Jerusalem. Yet there were obstacles. The time was not yet right.

"Soon, John," he said finally. "Until the time comes, it must be our secret."

But the time must come. He must go on crusade. It would be his way of the cross.

CHAPTER SIX

The Cross of Red

THE king, they said, was dying. In his great wide bed Louis lay and heard all the whisperings and weeping, and he could not open his eyes. He too believed he was dying. The illness was like a heavy, sickening cloud which took his breath away and pressed him hard against the serge sheet. A little while ago—he did not know how long—he had summoned his entire family and court and thanked them all for their services and attentions. He had received the Last Sacraments. He could hear Bishop William's voice saying the Rosary and other tear-choked voices answering. The cloud pressed so heavily that all his breath was gone. He was only thirty-four years old—and he was dying. Now he would never go on crusade.

Crusade! Into the darkness of his closed eyes there swam a vision of himself, well and strong, mounted on a white charger with the oriflamme bright above his head. Egypt, the Nile, the infidels screaming out from the desert and the king's men charging to drive them back—he saw it so plainly. Egypt, not Palestine, was the place to start a crusade! Strike at the enemy's home country! If the Lord would spare him, he would go to Egypt!

"He is dead! The king is dead!" he heard a woman wail. "Cover his face with the sheet!"

"He is not dead!" That was Marguerite's voice. Louis tried to answer, but neither sound nor motion came.

"The soul is still within his body," she sobbed. "Do not touch him!"

Suddenly the cloud broke. The vision disappeared. With a great sigh, the king stretched his arms and moved his head. An excited sobbing rose throughout the room. He opened his eyes. Blanche and Marguerite were beside his bed. Weakly he struggled to sit up. Marguerite slipped her arm under his shoulders, raising him.

"The Lord," he said in a voice that did not sound like his own, "the Lord has brought me back from the dead. He has brought me back for a purpose, and by His grace I shall accomplish it!"

The effort of speaking was so great that the blackness fell over him again, but he forced himself to finish.

"I will take the cross of crusade!"

Complete silence fell upon the room. Blanche, who had been sitting on the edge of the bed, slipped to her knees.

"No, no!" she whispered.

"Give me the cross of crusade!" Louis urged. "Quickly!"

"Let him have it, Bishop William!" Marguerite begged. "He is so ill he must not be denied!"

William took a crucifix from his belt and laid it in Louis' hand.

"The cross of crusade, my son. There it is!"

Joy welled like the illness, overwhelming in its weight. But Louis knew that from that moment on, he would gain in health.

The weeks of recovery were long, and it was

autumn before the king again brought up the subject of crusade. He was resting in his chamber after the midday meal as had become his habit. Today he had summoned his family and the Bishop of Paris. Not since the day he so nearly died had they all been assembled. Their sober expressions told that they knew the reason for this meeting. Marguerite played nervously with the sash of her dress. Robert, Charles and Alphonse stood together as if for once they agreed.

The queen mother sat on the foot of the bed, severely commanding.

"I have been thinking, Louis," she said, "that now you are well enough for a journey. I am arranging for us to go down into the south of France to collect our taxes."

"No, Mother," the king said quietly. "We must not begin to eat our way through the kingdom in the fall. Spring is the time for that."

But he smiled. The tax-collecting jaunts were like a perpetual picnic, with the king's whole party lingering along while they ate up the cheese and bread owed by the peasants.

"I am going on another journey, Madame. You remember that I have taken the cross."

He held up the crucifix he had received

from William. Marguerite began to cry. The queen mother turned pale as death. Bishop William, with a great effort, rose to his feet.

"My lord, we are happy to hear of your pious wish," he said, "but when you received the cross you had just awakened from the sleep of the dead and you were not of sound mind. Such a vow is not binding."

"It is binding if I make it so now."

"France has always been first with you, my lord! The peace of the kingdom depends on you. Frederick of Germany threatens us on one side, Henry of England on the other. Leave the kingdom now and I could not answer for what it might be on your return!"

"My mother can rule again as well as she did during my minority." Louis turned to Marguerite. "What do you say, my dear?"

The young queen swallowed a sob. "I say, Louis, that you must remember you have a wife and children!"

"I shall remember by taking them with me."

"Oh, then go! Go!"

Louis was a little embarrassed. Marguerite need not show so plainly how happy she would be to get away from his mother.

"And you, Madame?" he asked. "Do I have your blessing?"

The queen mother arose. She was beautiful as she had ever been, but her face was drawn with anxiety.

"My son, I have always given you good counsel, have I not?"

"Could anyone doubt it, Madame?"

"Then believe me when I say that a good, obedient son is pleasing to God. I bid you give up this idea of crusade!"

"And leave the Holy Land in the hands of the infidel?"

"Together you and I will raise an army, more men-at-arms than you could have led yourself. We'll send them to the Holy Land. But not you, my son! Not you!"

Never in his life would Louis do so difficult a thing as he was about to do now. Rising with a great effort from the bed, he stood before the bishop. But he spoke first to his mother.

"Madame, I love you with the true devotion of a son and with the loyalty and admiration of a subject for a beloved ruler. But I love God more." Turning to the bishop, he continued, "You have just stated, my lord bishop, that I was not of sound mind when I took the cross. Here, I return it to you."

He held out the crucifix. William took it.

"You have done well, my son!" Blanche exclaimed.

Louis went shakily to his knees before the bishop.

"Now I ask for the cross back again. Fix it to my shoulder!"

William, hesitating, looked at the queen mother.

"I swear that not one crumb of bread shall I eat until the cross is mine!" Louis declared.

In utter silence, William bent and with trembling hands pinned the cross in place. As soon as it was done, Robert, Charles and Alphonse strode across the room and lifted Louis strongly to his feet. Then, arm in arm, all four stood together to face the company.

"We go with the king!" Robert said firmly. "If our brother Philip had lived, he also would be with us. We go together!"

Louis could only smile. It was the first time his brothers had presented a solid front with him against their mother.

Through the weeks that followed, it seemed to the king that everywhere he went, he heard talk against crusade. The time for crusading was over; disease and degrading habits were brought back from the East; such an undertaking was merely a chance for young, idle noblemen to escape the boredom of home. But against these arguments were others. A marvelous brotherhood was born amongst the crusaders, for on the field of battle a peasant was the equal of a count. Heroism flourished at least as well as barbarism. Most important of all, a man had an opportunity to spend his strength for God instead of for a worldly purpose.

Young John of Joinville sent word that he would be with the king. At court, however, there was little enthusiasm. So Louis resorted to a sort of holy practical joke.

On Christmas morning he was up even earlier than usual. The knights who slept in his chamber awoke, saw in the dim light of the one candle that the king was being dressed, and straggled up from their pallets with a great deal of yawning and eye-rubbing. In their robing room they would not bother to light candles. Their sleepy squires would present them with the new mantles which the king, as lord of the household, must furnish every Christmas, and without being conscious of anything more than the feel of the new taffeta they would stumble along to the chapel.

It happened exactly as Louis expected. In the dark chapel everyone was too sleepy to be discerning; but as daylight filtered through the stained glass windows, the knights glanced admiringly and then in dismay at one another's new mantles. On the shoulder of each was embroidered the red cross of promised crusade.

Coming out of the chapel, the knights began to laugh and joke with their king for the way he had tricked them, some of the laughter not too happy. But Louis was satisfied. Now he had an army.

From the nucleus of crusaders at court, the interest spread. All over France the barons began exhorting their people to prepare the provisions for the long journey. The king himself undertook such a project of justice as had never been heard of before. Assembling a great horde of marshals who were known for their strict justice, he sent them into all parts of the kingdom. Then he invited people of every rank from low to high to come before these judges with any grievance or injustice which dated back even into the time of Philip Augustus, and the wrong would be made right.

"I cannot go forth on crusade until I know that all wrongs have been righted at home," Louis insisted many times during the two years it took for this enormous wheel of justice to complete its turning.

At the end of that time, no one could complain that his interests had been slighted. Other preparations also were made. Crops of wheat were planted, ships were built, and the army itself grew until every family in France could boast of at least a cousin who would go to Egypt with the king. For that course, at Louis' insistence, had finally been settled upon: meet the Saracens, who were the most powerful antagonists in the Holy Land, upon their own ground, and defeat them there. Then the holy places of Palestine would be easily taken. On Friday, June 12, 1248, when the king took his vow, the churches from Brittainy to Burgundy and down to the Pyrenees were filled with knights also taking the vow.

Barefooted, Louis walked with his brothers and a large company from court out to the Church of St. Denis. There he received the oriflamme which would be his banner until his return to France. From the abbot he also received the crusader's purse and the pilgrim's staff. Then, in appearance no different from the most humble squire, he walked back into the city to Notre Dame and heard Mass. If ever earthly happiness could be his lot, it belonged to him now.

The Mass ended, the people left the cathedral, but the king went on praying. When he arose finally, only one knight remained with him in the great, still place. John of Joinville. The young lord looked older than his years. In silence he grasped the hand which Louis held out to him.

"You're not ill, John?" the king asked.

"Ill with farewells, Sire."

Louis' heart went heavy. He had been praying for the success of the crusade. He had forgotten the painful leave-takings.

"Three days ago I left Joinville," the young knight said. "Not once did I even turn my eyes in the direction of home for fear I might grow faint and return to my wife and two children. I have paid all my debts and I am almost penniless. I am depending on God as never before."

"And we are all serving God as never before," the king said gently. "If we feel that we sacrifice much, then we must remember that a sacrifice is the giving up of a good thing in order that we may gain something better."

His own words on sacrifice came back to Louis when he said good-by to his mother. She was now regent again. She accompanied the crusaders down into Burgundy to the town of Cluny, then on the short distance to the point on the River Saône where the party would embark on boats. The early June morning was warm, but Blanche appeared to be shivering as she stood with Louis at the river's edge. Around them was the clamor of a thousand shouting men, the heavy tramp of horses and the thump of provisions being loaded on the boats.

"My son," she said, "you have given me complete power to rule in your absence, and I will spare no effort. If God should call me before your return, then remember that I have loved you above all my children. And never has a son been more worthy."

She kissed him on the forehead. Her lips were cold. Quickly Louis jumped aboard the boat and the oarsmen pulled out into the current. When he looked back, he saw that his mother had fainted in the arms of her ladies-in-waiting. Marguerite came and sat with him, but he could not speak. At that moment he would almost gladly have returned to Paris.

The boats made a colorful passage, aflutter with banners and the sun striking fire from all the armor. Beside the boats, on the banks, the great war horses were led along. Down the Saône to the Rhone and thence down to Aigues-Mortes on the Mediterranean the crusaders went. The small town could not hold them. Louis took up residence in a very humble house.

Tents were erected for his brothers and their retinue, making a city in themselves. The tent city grew as other crusaders poured in from all over France. Preparations for departure were carried on from dawn to midnight, and by the twentieth of August thirty-eight ships and many more vessels of transport lay in the harbor. Any day now, whenever the master mariners should decide the wind was right for sailing, the fleet would depart.

At last on Friday, August 25, the master mariners were all agreed. Louis went to the small church of Notre Dame des Sablons to hear Mass, then waited on shore while the war horses were led into the hold of his ship as it stood high in the water. When the door was caulked up, watertight since it would be submerged once the ship was out of port, the king and his party went aboard.

"Are you ready?" the master mariner cried to the seamen in the prow.

"Yes, Sire!"

He turned to the king. "My lord, summon your priests and monks to the deck, for we are about to weigh anchor!"

Louis sent a page running below. In a few minutes the deck was crowded.

"Now sing, Fathers!" the master mariner cried.

The old hymn, "Veni Creator," was started by one voice, picked up by others, then went rolling over the bay until every ship was enfolded in a great wave of sound.

"How can we fail?" Louis asked aloud.

No one answered, for the master mariner had cried out, "Unfurl the sails, in the Name of God!" and the canvas was going up. All over the ships men were murmuring prayers and calling good-bys to families left ashore. The horses in the hold, feeling the first shudder of movement in the ship, fell to tramping and neighing.

In a few minutes the wind filled the sails. It was a good wind, and the ships were borne straight out to sea. Louis, looking over nothing but water, turned to his brother Robert.

"Now I know better than ever that I did right to set everything in order at home before I left. No man could face such peril as this with any wrong left behind him."

Robert nodded soberly, his high spirits for once chastened.

"Only God knows whether we shall end up on the farther shore or at the bottom of the sea," Louis added.

He missed Robert's reply. He was straining his vision toward the southeast, as if already he could make out the sandy desert beaches of Egypt.

CHAPTER SEVEN

The Sands of Egypt

THE wind blew fair across the Mediterranean, and the great fleet sailed steadily past Sardinia and Sicily. Staying well out from the dangerous Barbary Coast held by the Saracens, then away from the Island of Crete, they landed at Cyprus on September 12. For two years the king's envoys had been in Cyprus buying up supplies, and now along the shore there were casks of wine stacked as high as barns, and mountains

of wheat and barley which had sprouted themselves a green cover in the rains.

The king, seeing all this from the deck of the
Montjoie, was well satisfied.

"My men have bought provisions enough for
a year in Egypt!" he exclaimed to Robert.
"We can push on without delay!"

"The barons wish to remain in Cyprus for
the winter," Robert said.

"Why?" Louis asked somewhat shortly, for
he had heard rumblings of this idea. "Why
should we give the Saracens warning and time
to prepare for an invasion?"

"We must wait at least for our allies to join
us," Robert reminded him. "Many of them are
far behind."

"We will strike with those who are here!"
the king declared.

But he could not carry his will against the
solid opposition of the nobles. None would
stand with him. The King of Cyprus, who had
not known that he would be called upon to be
host to so many hundreds, nevertheless showed
warm hospitality. He would even join the
crusade, he said, but not until his people had
time to raise a crop of wheat for his own army.

"And in the meantime his realm will profit
from the lavish spending of my men!" Louis

stated impatiently to the council of war. "I will not wait a year! It is folly to sit here while the enemy prepares to resist us!"

Yet, for all his impatience, it was eight months later, after a winter beset by all the annoyances that come from idleness, that the crusaders once again went aboard their ships. Through the long winter so many others had joined them that over eighteen hundred ships set out from Cyprus. The blue water looked as if it had sprouted white wings. There was singing again, and an uproar of master mariners calling out to one another to mind carefully how their oarsmen steered because the ships rode so close together.

"Follow! Follow the king!" the master mariner cried from the *Montjoie*, and the cry was carried from end to end of the armada. Louis, hearing it, gave thanks again. At last he was attempting the real crusade.

One more anchorage was made off the south coast of Cyprus. Some of the nobles with their vassals had passed the winter in Greece and they had been sent word that the Point of Limassol would be the meeting place. On Pentecost Sunday, which was May 21 in 1249, Louis went ashore to hear Mass. Toward the end of the Mass the sky blackened with storm clouds, and the crusaders had barely reached their ships when the wind struck. All canvas was lashed down tightly, yet when the storm had spent itself, a mere seven hundred of the fleet remained.

"We have lost over a thousand of our ships!" Louis exclaimed sorrowfully to the master mariner.

"Not lost them, my lord. They are blown to the shores of Palestine, but they are too well built to be at the bottom of the sea. They will join us again, Sire."

But the king knew as well as the master mariner that weeks and even months might pass before the fleet would be whole again, if ever.

"We cannot wait," Louis decreed. "As soon as the wind is right, set sail for Egypt."

The next day the wind was right, and after four days of sailing, the wide green delta of the Nile seemed to rise out of the sea. There was a glitter to it, as if the sun struck fire out of the sand. As his galley neared the shore Louis saw that the streaks of light shot from the breastplates of armored soldiers.

"Gold!" Robert exclaimed. "The sultan's arms are all of gold! And listen to those golden cymbals!"

"Hardly a golden sound!" said Louis, for

the din of cymbals and horns was fearful to hear. The soldiers presented a solid front with their shields fixed in the sand, their ranks extending as far as the eye could see.

"There must be six thousand!" Robert cried. "We would make perfect targets for their arrows while we are helpless, landing."

"Tell the master mariner to drop anchor," Louis said. "And have him summon all the principal leaders aboard this ship. We'll take counsel among ourselves."

The barons, putting out in small boats from their galleys, arrived sober-faced. Over on the shore the clamor died a little, as if the enemy waited now to see what would happen. But the bowmen still remained shoulder to shoulder behind their wall of shields.

"How can we defeat such an army?" the Duke of Burgundy demanded loudly enough for the king to hear. "They far outnumber us!"

Louis arose from the place where he had been sitting in the shadow of a sail. They were all together, his own brothers, Peter and Hugh who had opposed him in France, others who had stood with him, all gathered now in one brotherhood. Each time they faced the enemy in battle, a few would lie dead on the sands.

This was the last hour on earth that all would be together.

"My friends good and true," Louis said slowly, "if we are bound together in our love of one another, nothing can defeat us. God has shown us His approval of our undertaking in enabling us to come so far. Now that we are almost on the shores of the Saracen land, let us not lose heart."

He paused, looking over the crowd. "I am not now the King of France. I am one of you, a man who will die like other men in God's good time. If we die on this crusade, we will be martyrs and go straight to heaven. If we are victorious, then it will be for the glory of God and of all Christendom. God saved my life for this purpose, and whatever the outcome of the crusade, He will triumph in us, not for us. Blessed be His holy name!"

"Blessed be God!" the men murmured.

"Now say what you will. Shall we land and fight the forces of the sultan?"

"Not yet, Sire," said the Duke of Burgundy. "We shall need all the strength we can muster. Wait for those who were blown away in the storm."

"Sit here for a year listening to the sultan's

racket?" Robert jeered. "I say let us attack this very moment!"

"We cannot anchor close to shore," the master mariner put in. "There are sandbars too dangerous for the big galleys."

"The small boats can carry us," said the Count of Jaffa. "And the horses can swim in through the shallow water. Attack and show the sultan we are not afraid!"

"Who spoke of being afraid?" Burgundy demanded angrily. "I am cautious, not fearful!"

A few heads nodded, but the barons for the most part were no longer with the duke. None had moved, yet there was the definite feeling of drawing together around the king.

"Damietta is a city so important to the Saracens," Louis said quietly, "that its fall would mean the tottering of their power. Does anyone argue that we should not take it?"

"No, no, Sire," the barons murmured.

"The city lies eight miles up the delta. If we are to wait, where would we drop anchor? There is no port here, no harbor. On the open sea we are at the mercy of the wind. We cannot risk having our ships blown away again to other lands. We must take Damietta." The king paused a moment. The emblem of St. Denis flapped above his head. "We attack at dawn tomorrow. And may God grant us victory in His name!"

"Amen!" Robert exclaimed so heartily that most of the men smiled.

Louis did not sleep that night. He remained on deck, praying. The sweeps lay motionless in the water like the legs of some big quiet bug. Over on shore the Saracens were silent. A few campfires burned brightly, going out just before dawn when the priest lighted the candles to say Mass aboard the *Montjoie*. Louis prayed as he never had before. These next hours would almost determine the success or failure of the entire crusade. If the Saracens should repulse them, he would have a hard time convincing the crusaders that they should try again.

Since the galleys could not put in to shore because of the sandbars, all of the armed men and the horses must be taken in small boats. It would make a slow landing, wide open to attack. The moon had gone down, the cover of darkness was complete; yet at the first movement of the small boats, the din broke out again on shore.

"So they are awake to welcome us!" Robert cried. "Very well, pagans, we come!"

"With all speed!" Louis added, for to him the noise was the call to battle. Running to the ship's prow, he called out to the master mariner, "Hold steady for land!"

The old mariner shook his head. "Remember the sandbars, Sire! We dare not go aground, not with the queen and your children aboard us!"

"I command you, steer straight for shore!"

The master mariner could not disobey, but he gave orders to have the sweeps touch the water so lightly that all the small boats, one by one, slipped past the *Montjoie*. When the big ship was only entering the rim of arrows shot by the Saracen bowmen, the boat carrying the oriflamme reached shore.

"The standard of St. Denis will not touch foreign soil without me!" Louis shouted.

Fully armed, with his shield before him and lance in hand, he scrambled over the ship's rail.

"My lord, do not do such a foolhardy thing!" a monk begged. "If you will not think of your own safety, think of your wife and children!"

But Louis had already leaped into the shallow water. A moment later Robert was with him, and the two waded together toward shore, protecting themselves with their shields against the arrows as best they could.

The water was thrashed into foam by hurry-

ing men and horses. Robert and Louis, sometimes losing their footing, helping each other
forward, reached the shore just as the banner
of St. Denis was being planted stoutly in the
sand.

"Forward!" Louis shouted, and he would
have rushed into a band of Saracens if he had
not been held bodily by his knights.

"We all must act under your command,
Sire!" the young Lord of Joinville shouted close
to his ear, for the racket was so loud that a
shout seemed like a whisper.

Louis stood still, panting, and thrust the
point of his shield deep into the sand. When he
saw the Saracens so close, he had been filled
with a terrible anger. These were the people
who had desecrated the Holy Land. But now
he wiped his face and leaned against the shield.
If all of his knights were to dash willy-nilly
into the fray, it would be a simple matter for
the Saracens to cut them down.

"Thank you, John," he said, although the
young man could not hear him. Remaining near
the oriflamme, he watched the battle. His men,
mounting their horses even before they reached
shore, charged with such courage that the enemy was plainly confused. Soon there were
breaks in the solid line of shields. Horses began

streaking away to a safe distance, at first singly, then in increasing numbers until it was a rout. The crusaders, relieved for the moment of defending themselves, gathered into an orderly line and charged again. Louis jumped on a horse and followed. The last he saw of the enemy was the great dust cloud they raised as they galloped away toward Damietta.

"It is victory!" he cried. "Victory! Glory be to God!"

And such a shout went up from his army that it echoed after the Saracens.

"Let us ride after them and finish them off!" Robert begged.

But Louis, more prudent since he had so nearly acted with too much haste himself, ordered his forces to remain where they were. Dispatching John of Joinville to ride with two squires toward Damietta to keep a watch on the enemy, he turned with his men to the sad task of seeing to the dead and wounded.

In the late afternoon, John returned. One of the small boats had been beached, and there Louis met his messenger.

"The town is deserted, my lord," the knight reported. "Not a Saracen remains to defend it."

"They have abandoned Damietta?" Louis

asked, unbelieving. "This could be a trap, John."

"I have myself been into the empty house of the sultan, Sire. We rode through every street and saw only a few dogs and chickens."

"But why, John? Why give us a city we could only have taken by famine?"

"Because they think the sultan is dead, my lord."

The nobles who were listening shook their heads.

"I do not know for myself that he is dead, Sire," John continued, "but the leader of their army sent three messages to the sultan by carrier pigeon, telling him we had landed, and he never received any answer. Perhaps the sultan is ill. But Damietta is empty."

Louis grouped his army and began to ride slowly and watchfully toward the city. They had covered only a mile or so when a messenger came galloping back.

"Smoke, my lord! Smoke blackens the sky above Damietta!"

"Then the Saracens have returned!" Robert exclaimed. "Ride, Louis! Engage them before they can assemble for defense!"

But the king was still cautious. Informed at all times by messengers who galloped back and forth, he led the army to within sight of the city. Above the bleached walls the smoke billowed black and thick.

"It is straw, my lord," said an old knight, "straw that makes the black smoke. They must be burning the bazaar, which would be like our market place."

"They are destroying the provisions," Louis said. "But they overlooked what would have been an even greater loss to us. Is that not a bridge of boats remaining across the river?"

"It is, my lord."

Louis smiled. "God does indeed mean for us to take Damietta! He leaves the front door open in welcome!"

Yet the king and his leaders still proceeded with care. Not until the advance guard brought word that the city had been searched did he permit the army to move forward.

Riding across the bridge which was laid from boat to boat, Louis felt his spirit singing. Through the gate in the white wall, on into sandy, dry streets blocked into odd turnings by the flat-roofed houses, the King of France led his men. The fire in the market place had died to embers and the desert wind drove the smoke away. Before a towering mosque, Louis drew up his horse. The round dome appeared to be of pure gold, the delicate colors of fine mosaic decorated the arches, and the pillars were of snow white marble.

Louis dismounted, took off his helmet and knelt in the dust.

"Here place the standard of St. Denis! In the name of Mary I take this first ground from the enemy! As soon as the mosque can be purified, let a Mass be said here in her honor!"

The men around him murmured amen. The oriflamme looked strange on the steps of a Turkish mosque. Up under the arches the pigeons cooed. A buzzard flung itself out of a palm tree, circled, and flapped away over the empty houses. All through the streets now was the beat of hoofs and the hollow clank of armor as the army filled the town. Thirty years before, King John and England had taken Damietta by famine. On this June day of 1249, Louis of France knelt to give solemn thanks that he had taken Damietta again, by the grace of God.

CHAPTER EIGHT

Greek Fire

Louis had expected to move quickly on from Damietta, but now more delays came upon the army. Residences must be found for Queen Marguerite and her ladies among the ruined houses and a guard established for them because it was decided that the women should remain in Damietta. Out on the plain around the city the army set up camp, surrounding themselves with heavy earthworks; for the Saracens had a cunning way of appearing from nowhere on their swift Arab horses, darting in among the tents and leaving headless bodies behind them. The sultan was said to be paying a good price for every crusader's head brought to him, and the raids were many. But behind the earthworks the army was safe. Once more the pointed banners of the knights and the blunt banners of the bannerets whipped in the desert winds.

The encampment had a permanence about it that Louis did not like. The nobles had taken to feasting, and the knights to jousting and merrymaking as if they were again in the heart of France. Calling the leaders together in his own tent, the king was blunt with them.

"We must not wait as we did in Cyprus while our host spends its money in revelry," he said. "By our delay the Saracens will only become stronger in number and in purpose while we become weaker. It is time to follow up our good victory with another!"

"Let us march on Alexandria," said Peter of Brittainy who was now one of the king's chief advisers. "It would give us a seaport for our ships and a good base for supplies."

"Not Alexandria," Robert objected, and when the nobles protested he went on, "Babylon, I say! It is the seat of Saracen power, the capital of Egypt. What is more reasonable than that we should take it?"

"Exactly!" Peter exclaimed. "That's just why we should *not* try to take it. It is what the enemy expects! Besides, Babylon lies far up the river from here. Our ships would have to follow us against the current of the Nile, and the Saracens would cut them to pieces on that slow passage!"

"Wait for our brother Alphonse," Robert said stubbornly. "With the fresh forces he is bringing from France, we can take Babylon."

The king listened with the intentness he always gave to his advisers. Then he turned to the Lord of Joinville.

"What think you, John?"

"I think we will never take Babylon! Between Babylon and Damietta lies Mansourah, a good fortress in itself, and the Saracens are using this time to make it better. Before we could even reach Mansourah we would have to cross a wide branch of the Nile where it divides to form the delta. A causeway would be our only means of crossing, and the enemy will hardly sit quietly while we build one. No, Sire, our strength would be spent for nothing if we were to march south."

Everyone but Robert murmured agreement.

Yet when the king's decision was made, it was in accord with Robert. The entire crusade would await Alphonse. Then the campaign to Babylon would be undertaken.

Almost three weeks went by before the French ships dropped anchor beyond the delta and Alphonse with his men came up to Damietta in small boats. On December 6, 1249, Louis ordered his forces to break camp and move south, leaving behind only the guard required to protect the women and children.

The first advance was short. The army encamped again, still on the delta. Behind them was the arm of the river known as the Stream of Damietta, before them was the Stream of Rexi. On the far bank of the Rexi the Saracen forces were drawn up, ready for battle.

"So now we swim across," said Robert as he sat his horse beside Louis and looked out over the river.

"We build a causeway," said the king. "But first we build covered walks to protect the men who must bring up the earth for the causeway."

"And to protect the walks, there must be cat castles?"

"Of course. The enemy will begin throwing stones with their engines as soon as we approach the river."

"What a time it will take!" the young prince said impatiently. "Swimming would be faster!" And he spurred his horse into an instant gallop, disappearing in a cloud of sand.

The king looked after him with some misgiving. Robert was as handsome a knight as could be seen, fair, tall as Louis himself. But in his gray eyes there was no serenity. He was like a falcon, poised to fly. Louis, walking slowly into his tent, wondered if perhaps he should have followed the unanimous advice of his barons. Robert, after all, was not a military leader. In the tent, the king knelt beside his cot and buried his head in his arms. He might not have good judgment as a general, but as a pilgrim, under God, he was walking in the straight way. There he had no doubt.

Ponderously the work went forward. First, eighteen heavy wooden engines were built to throw stones larger than could be handled by swivel bows. Then, at the river bank where the covered walks ended, two tall cat castles were erected and an engine mounted in each. Protected in this manner, the men went to work eagerly hauling up earth for the causeway. Darts and stones slung by the enemy made a continual hail around them, but the highway pushed steadily out into the river. The stream, however, never seemed to grow narrower; for as the causeway advanced, the Saracens dug away the bank on the farther side, keeping the river as wide as ever.

"We shall never cross this way," said old Peter of Brittany as he stood with the king watching the swirling current.

"How, then?" Louis asked.

"Find us a shallow place where we can ford the stream."

"We have hunted and found none." Louis squinted at the enemy forces a half mile away. "Peter, they are bringing up a petrary. What do they intend doing now?"

The petrary, another type of engine with a stout bow, was settled to face the causeway. It was almost midnight, however, before the king's question was answered. There was no moon, and the desert stars seemed to hang low as candles in a tall tree. Louis was pacing before his tent when the dark sky was suddenly lighted up by a ball of fire which came thundering straight toward the causeway. The entire camp was bright as day as the flaming thing hung above it. The king fell to his knees. And then the fire was falling, screaming like a devil as it plunged into the city of tents. Instantly, flames shot up.

"Lord of heaven, save my people!" Louis prayed aloud.

He was getting to his feet when the Lord of Joinville came running up.

"Sire, this is why they moved up the petrary! They are using it to throw the Greek fire!"

"Greek fire? Never have I seen such an instrument of the devil!" the king exclaimed.

Over where the fire had fallen, men were running, shouting garbled orders to one another. Horses screamed, breaking their tethers and galloping wildly among the tents.

"Stay here, Sire!" Joinville cried.

But the king was running with the others to help fight the flames. No sooner had the first blaze been put out than another bolt fell into the camp. At dawn there was a third, but with daylight the fiery onslaught ceased. Wearily the leaders gathered with the king to decide what should be done.

"Organize teams of firemen," said Joinville. "We must defend ourselves until the causeway is completed."

"Find a ford in the river so we can cross quickly," Peter urged.

"Swim across and run every Saracen through with a lance!" Robert cired.

Louis paid no heed to his brother. Peter's advice was already being followed, with men searching all day for a place to ford the river. It was Joinville who put the most practical scheme into operation. When the Greek fire began to fall again that night, the firemen were on guard all over the camp. But by dawn, the barrel-size shafts burned like a hedge along the waterfront, and both cat castles had caught fire but were salvaged without much damage.

Daylight brought no respite this time. The Saracens grew bolder, dragging their engines so close to the causeway that the defenders had to leave their building and take refuge out of range of the stones and the Greek fire. Both cat castles were burned to the ground. The King of Sicily, who was in charge of the day-time defense, had to be restrained from running to put out the fires with his bare hands. Many of the crusaders sat down and wept like children.

"Are we to end our crusade here on the bank of the Rexi?" they asked hopelessly.

Even now, Louis was not discouraged.

"We have one course left," he told his barons. "In our boats there is good wood. Let

us take enough from each to build us one
more tower."

"How can we return to our galleys out on
the sea if we destroy our small boats, Sire?" the
Count of Jaffa argued. "Let us at least keep a
way of escape!"

Louis saw agreement among all his lords.
Even John of Joinville did not stand with him
now. But how could he give up?

"We build the tower," he said. "Right or
wrong, I am still your king."

The tower was built. The Saracens shot
Greek fire upon it and burned it to the ground.

The river still ran wide and deep with no
apparent crossing. The enemy ranks so far out-
numbered the king's forces that they could be
changed continually for rested men, and the
tired crusaders were no match for them. Supplies soon would be running low. Tents lay in
charred ruins, carcasses of horses were swelling
on the river bank. Yet Louis was not discouraged. In the shelter of his tent he prayed
all the hours he was not out with his men,
never resting.

No one seeing the Bedouin ride up dirty and
black-bearded could guess that he held the
answer to the king's prayers. His long gown
was tan with dust, the folds of his head scarf

filled with sand. The constable on guard stopped him with drawn sword. The Bedouins, nomads of the desert, were loyal to the Saracens only because they were paid as soldiers. With rough gestures the man made it plain to the constable that if the king would pay him more than the Saracens were paying, he would lead the army to a ford in the river.

Louis heard the news with delight. The man was paid. Then, so hastily that some of their equipment was left behind, the crusaders followed him upstream to a part of the river that looked exactly like any other part. But the Bedouin's small Arab horse plunged in confidently, wading to midstream, then swimming for a short distance until the water became shallow again. When horse and rider came up safely on the far side, the crusaders gave a great cheer.

"Louis, let me cross first with my men and guard the ford!" Robert begged. "Let us carry the banner of St. Denis!"

"It is our right to carry the banner!" argued the Grand Master of the Templars. "Our order was founded for the defense of the Holy Land! We belong at the head of the army!"

The king could not bring himself to deny Robert.

"The Knights of the Temple shall be first,"
he said. "But you, Robert, will have the second
division after them. You shall carry the banner."

There was no murmuring. The Templars on
their heavy war horses headed into the stream.
Immediately after them came Robert proudly
escorting the oriflamme.

But on the farther side, order suddenly took
wing. The Saracens, seeing their enemies at last
touching ground they held to be theirs, made a
quick charge upon the Templars.

"Fall upon the heathens!" Robert cried, and
with his troops after him he swung around the
Knights of the Temple and plunged into the
enemy ranks. The dumfounded Saracens scattered to the horizon where they drew up in a
long line between the river and the town of
Mansourah.

"Your place was to come after us!" the
Grand Master shouted angrily to Robert.

"Then let us attack them instantly, together!"

"No! We wait for the king!"

"If you are afraid, you can stay behind!"
the young prince said impudently.

William Longsword, the chief of the English
crusaders, urged his horse between Robert and
the Grand Master.

"My lord Robert, we are not afraid. If you go, we follow. But I dare say, if we go we shall all soon be in heaven."

A messenger galloped up and pulled his mount to its haunches. "The king orders you to wait!" he cried.

But an old knight who had been Robert's tutor back in Paris and was so deaf he heard nothing, now caught the bridle of the prince's horse.

"Forward and send them to Purgatory!" he cried in his cracked old voice.

Robert needed no more urging. With his men after him, he streaked toward the line of Saracens waiting on the horizon. The Templars, not to be outdone, pounded behind.

As he reached the bank of the river, Louis saw the fanatical charge. The Saracens, no doubt thinking the whole Christian army was upon them, were routed and galloping off toward Mansourah. Robert and his men disappeared into the sandy cloud that hid the enemy.

The king commanded the army to follow. But the fording of the river was slow. Louis would not wait. Galloping on, he found himself suddenly in the midst of six Arabs. One seized his horse's bridle. With furious strokes of his sword he freed himself just as his own knights rushed up.

"Onward!" Louis cried.

Robert had chased the enemy into Mansourah and out on the other side, but now they rallied and descended again upon the crusaders. The battle was a tumult of flashing swords and darting lances, all made more terrifying by the continuous clashing of cymbals and blowing of horns with which the Saracens confused their opponents.

By sundown the enemy had fled. On the field of battle lay the engines of war with which the enemy had thrown the Greek fire, and many of their tents. Everywhere were the dead and the wounded. Louis, looking over the field, was joined by the Grand Master of the Knights of Malta.

"What of my brother Robert?" the king asked. "Is he well entrenched in Mansourah?"

The knight took off his helmet and rested it on the saddle before him. "Robert, Count of Artois, is in paradise."

The king could not reply. After a moment the knight went on. "He died bravely, Sire. He could not keep Mansourah. Three hundred knights are dead. And the Master of the Temple tells me he lost fourteen score men-at-arms and all their horses."

"My brothers Charles and Alphonse?" Louis asked. "And Lord John of Joinville?"

"My lord, your brothers are well. John is badly hurt."

The king could bear no more. He mounted his horse. The oriflamme, ripped by a lance, hung lifeless in the evening air. Out over the battlefield the sun shone with sunset brightness, but it struck no fire from shields or armor. All the shining metal was dulled with blood and sand.

"We have won the victory," the knight said after a moment.

"Yes, and let us thank God for all His goodness to us."

But when Louis rode away, he could not see where his horse went because of the great tears that blinded him.

CHAPTER NINE

Prison!

THE barons urged that the army return to Damietta and leave their perilous stand on the open field before Mansourah, which again belonged to the Saracens. The battlefield was disease-ridden because the dead were buried in shallow trenches and the river water was polluted. But the king again was adamant. He refused to retreat.

"We do not give up ground we have bought so dearly," he said. "Surround the camp with palisades and set a guard day and night. When the sick are well again, we move forward."

The palisades, made of long pointed stakes set close together, were an indifferent defense. The Saracens were continually charging the camp on foot or horseback, squeezing between the stakes to sling their bolts and arrows and escaping with almost no loss. Three days after the great battle, on the eleventh of February, another smaller encounter took place just outside the camp. The crusaders fought with such desperation that the attack turned into a rout.

Still, in spite of two victories, the situation of the army was dangerous. Louis, helping to nurse the sick, fell ill himself. Calling his leaders together, he lay on his cot, weak and pale.

"My brothers, we left Damietta with nearly forty thousand men," he said. "Now, with illness and loss in battle, we must consider only that we can defend ourselves against the enemy, not attack them. We cannot remain here much longer, for the Saracens grow bolder. So we must use strategy other than the sword."

Louis had to wait for strength to go on. "Today I have sent a message to the new sultan, Malek-Moaddam. I offered to leave Egypt and give up Damietta if he will return Jerusalem to the Christians and permit all of

us to board our ships without danger. The
messenger has come back with a reply. I summoned you to hear it."

In the expectant silence, a fully armored
knight stepped into the circle from the doorway where he had been waiting.

"Speak!" the king said weakly.

"The sultan was pleased, Sire. But—my lord,
he demands you as a hostage! Not one of your
brothers, as you offered, but yourself!"

An angry murmur arose among the barons.
They did not have to take counsel as to how
to receive this insolence. John of Joinville,
pale and thin, with one shoulder wrapped in a
ragged bandage, spoke out before the others.

"Sire, let Malek-Moaddam slay us all rather
than take you in pawn!"

The king smiled again. "I am a man like you,
John. If my poor body can serve as a guarantee
for safe passage of the army—"

But Joinville was so incensed that he interrupted the king, a thing no man ever did.

"We shall not return to France with heads
bowed in shame because we left our most
Christian king in the hands of the infidel!"

Louis lay back on his cot. The warm affection of these fighting men washed over him
like a healing ointment. Some of them had

taken up arms against him in France, but they would lay down their lives for him on the sands of Egypt.

"We shall retreat," he said weakly. "It is not a surrender, merely a withdrawal back to Damietta, where we can rest and plan. Tell the constables and the masters-at-arms to prepare for immediate departure."

On the fifth day of April, in the early morning, the tents were struck and the slow removal of the sick to the boats was begun. Ill as he was, the king had spent all his days going from one to another of the hospital tents, and now he was so weak he could hardly sit his horse. He had come to Egypt a tall, handsome knight with eager eyes and gay courage. Now he sat the small Arab horse like an old man, his shoulders so bowed that he had lost his height, his cheeks hollow and his eyes dull but still with the serenity of perfect resignation to the will of God. His hair had fallen from the fever and hung not in the golden waves but in short strings to his shoulders.

"Sire, you are so ill, go aboard a boat with the sick!" Joinville urged.

The king looked at the knight's drawn face and the ragged bandage. "Will you go aboard a boat, John?"

"No, Sire. But that is different!"

Louis only smiled. Remaining upon the battlefield, he watched the last of the sick carried away and saw the remnant of his army mount their horses. At times he held hard to his saddle to keep from falling. At last, joining the rear guard under Geoffrey of Sargines, with the faithful Joinville beside him, he rode away from the field that had seen both victory and disaster for his army. The Saracens, always on watch, harassed the retreating host at every step, swarming especially around the king.

"You fight them off like flies when they buzz around the wine cup," Louis said, for each time an enemy approached, the two knights ran him off with their spears.

Clutching the silk housing which covered his mount, Louis fought back waves of blackness until he knew he could ride no farther.

"There is a small village up ahead," said Joinville. "Take him there, Geoffrey. I'll gather some knights and come to defend you."

Afterwards, Louis could never recall the ride into the village. When once more he knew where he was, he was lying on the floor of a room with charred walls, his head in the lap of a woman who had come with her husband from Paris. She was crying, Louis saw. She must think he was going to die. He did not think so himself.

Outside the house he could hear the clank of armor and the shouts of men. Joinville had indeed gathered a guard. From the sound, every man except the sick had turned back into the village.

Young Lord Philip of Montfort entered and knelt beside the king with a gourd of water.

"Sire, I have seen the emir with whom we talked of the truce before," Philip said. "If it is still your wish, I shall go to him and tell him that we will agree to leave you as hostage until our safe embarkation on our ships out at sea. You are in great peril here. No worse could befall you at the hands of the Saracens. Indeed, they would treat you well since you would not be a prisoner but a royal hostage."

"Go!" Louis breathed weakly. "Make the truce quickly!"

The king lay back. The woman dipped her scarf in water and bathed his face. When there was a loud shouting outside and four Saracens entered, one of them lifting him in his arms, Louis believed for a moment that the truce had been concluded. But when he was borne outside and saw his men disarmed and the Saracens milling among them, he knew that something very wrong had happened.

Lord Philip had gone to the emir, who had taken off his turban from his head and his ring from his finger, signifying that he would respect the truce which Philip proposed. But even while Lord Philip was talking with the emir, a treacherous sergeant named Marcel, who was secretly in the pay of the Saracens, leaped from his horse to the high rim of a well.

"The king commands us to surrender!" he shouted. "He will be killed unless we surrender! Throw down your swords and lances!"

None of the crusaders knew of the truce talk. They obeyed Marcel. The Saracens rushed in. When the emir, only a short distance off, saw that the crusaders were being taken prisoner, he hastily wrapped his turban around his head, put on his ring, and took Philip prisoner like the rest.

All through the village now there was confusion. Down on the river the boats carrying the sick battled a wind that blew straight against them from Damietta. Saracens leaped from the bank to the boats, killing and wounding those already ill. The knights who guarded the boats were bound with cords. When the king was carried aboard the sultan's own galley, all of the crusaders including his own brothers were lined on the river bank, dismounted and their hands tied behind them.

The king lay on a silk-covered couch and listened to Geoffrey's account of Marcel's treachery. Horns blasted joyfully over the royal prisoner. On the shore only a few yards beyond the sweeps of the galley, Charles and Alphonse toiled along, their cords replaced with chains.

"In Thine own good time, Thou shalt deliver us," Louis murmured. God had not made things easy even for His own Son.

The king was transported up the river like a prisoner of state, but at Mansourah the good treatment ended. There he was thrown into a dungeon and loaded with chains so heavy that in his illness he could scarcely move. All of his clothes were taken away and he wore only a surtout which a servant had taken from his own back. One old attendant was left to him, Ysambert who had come with him from Paris. With great affection and sympathy the servant cared for the king, cooking the scant food given them, trying to ease the weight of the chains, answering what he knew of the prayers Louis was constantly saying.

Outside the door the Saracen guard listened to the praying.

"Is he making curses against the sultan?" he asked Ysambert in his own tongue.

Ysambert had picked up enough of the Saracen dialect so he could reply. "My lord prays to the one true God to deliver us."

"I have never guarded anyone so quiet," the man said. "Even when he is forced to look upon the torture of his men, he does not complain. Why does he not beat the walls and cry out?"

"Because his imprisonment is the will of God."

"The sultan took him prisoner, not God!"

Ysambert shook his head. "The sultan could not have touched our king if God had not so willed it."

The guard pushed a small book between the bars.

"I found it," he said.

Ysambert picked up the book. "I have seen it often in the king's hands! Where did you find it?"

The guard, perhaps feeling he was being too friendly, would not answer.

"My breviary! My precious breviary!" Louis said when Ysambert gave him the book. "God has not forgotten us! Prop me up so I can read from it!"

The servant wept over his master's joy.

The word of Louis' patient endurance filtered out from the prison. From time to time strange faces would peer in through the bars at this man who never complained. One day the guard flung wide the barred door, entered and began to open the locks on the king's chains.

"They are setting you free, my lord!" Ysambert exclaimed joyfully.

But the king was not set free. He was moved to better quarters. There was a window large enough to let in air, and there was no water on the floor.

In what appeared to be the afternoon, because a small shaft of sunlight fell through the window, the sultan himself came to the prison. Malek-Moaddam was a huge man, handsome, bearded and young. He wore many yards of orange silk wrapped in folds about him from head to foot, and from under the turban his black eyes seemed to flash fire. Striding to the middle of the floor, he regarded Louis for a long moment. The king, lying on his cot, returned the look calmly.

"I come to treat with you as an equal," he said in good French. When he had waited long enough for a reply and received none, the sultan asked arrogantly, "Are you not interested in a truce?"

"You have not spoken of a truce."

"I ask the immediate surrender of Damietta, five hundred thousand livres ransom, and the restoration of several places in Palestine still held by the Christians."

Louis hesitated only a moment. "My wife and children are in Damietta. You must guarantee their safety. As for the ransom, that is heavy, but I will pay it gladly for my followers. A king cannot be ransomed with money. For my own liberty I will give back Damietta. But I have no power over the cities of Palestine. You must deal with their conquerors, whoever they may be."

The sultan's handsome face was scornful. "I will rule all of Palestine! If you will not negotiate as I wish, then I shall talk with your principal barons!"

"I have ordered them not to talk with you. I alone will settle."

"Then I'll have them beheaded!"

"They will obey me."

Louis spoke as quietly as if he were discussing the weather. The sultan, impressed against his will, said defiantly, "If you will not be reasonable, I'll send you to the Grand Caliph of Baghdad who will keep you prisoner for the rest of your life!"

"I am your prisoner," said the king. "You may do with me as you wish."

Angrily the sultan wheeled, and his silk robes swished as he strode to the door. There he turned, to look back at Louis with respect.

"You say you are my prisoner. I thought so, indeed. But you treat me as if I were your defeated enemy!"

The respect bore fruit. The same day, word was brought to Louis that the sultan himself would pay one hundred thousand livres of the ransom.

The treaty was concluded, and on the first of May, 1250, the prison gates were opened and the king and his men moved out to travel, some by land and some by boat, to within sight of Damietta. There, surrounded by a heavy guard of Saracens, they camped. The sultan, who had accompanied his men, would meet with the king to decide on the final details of the surrender of the city.

But while Louis sat with his nobles awaiting the arrival of the sultan, several emirs rode up with swords drawn, leaped from their horses and ran into the king's tent.

"Do not be afraid!" the leader cried to the astounded barons. "We have just slain Malek-Moaddam! He was our enemy and yours. He would have had you beheaded as soon as you gave up Damietta. What will you give us for his heart?"

Louis answered quietly, "I want no part of murder. Who will be your sultan now?"

"You, my lord! We will name you our sultan if you will make us all knights!"

The barons gasped, but the king showed no surprise. "I shall do so gladly if you will become Christians first."

"Christians? Ha!" The emir struck his own chest with a sword that left a red smear. "You cannot leave Egypt unless we permit it!"

"I know that," Louis replied.

With a gruff order to his men, the emir left the tent.

"Sire, why did you not agree to anything he proposed until we have our freedom?" Peter of Brittany urged.

"Do you mean I should have made knights of those infidels merely to save our skins? Never!"

The barons said no more. That night all of the army were again taken prisoner by the emirs, and only after the leaders were satisfied that Louis would respect the truce and leave Egypt did they agree to withdrawal. Even while the talks went on, other hosts stormed the walls of Damietta. Queen Marguerite, who had just given birth to a son, called an old knight to her and made him promise to take her life rather than permit her and her tiny baby to fall into the hands of the infidels. But the swarming hordes were turned back at the walls they themselves had built, and a few hours later the king and his men entered the gates. The queen and her children and her ladies were immediately put aboard the galleys.

Twenty thousand Saracens guarded the river, taking care that no ship should leave until the ransom money had been counted. From early Saturday morning until late Sunday night the money was weighed in the balance, the Saracen method of counting. Then the French ships were released to sail down the river.

Marguerite stood on the deck of the galley with her baby in her arms. The king was with her. He looked tired and old, but there was about him a great peace.

"What have you named our son?" he asked, laying his finger in the tiny curled fist.

"John Tristram, my lord, Tristram for sorrow because he was born in such an unhappy time." The queen, hesitating, asked timidly, "We are setting sail now for home, Louis?"

A beautiful smile lighted the king's face. "Home? Yes, my dear." He looked out over the calm blue waters of the Mediterranean. "Yes, now we sail home—to the Holy Land!"

CHAPTER TEN

The Holy Land

ON the fourteenth of May, 1250, after a calm journey, the crusaders' fleet arrived before St. Jean d'Acre, a port which remained in the hands of the Christians. There was glad rejoicing on the part of the residents, who received the king's party with open arms. Comfortable houses were given over to them, and their manner of living became luxurious in comparison to what they had endured at Mansourah. Yet it soon became plain to Louis that many of the nobles wished to return home. There was also an urgent message from his mother.

The king called his barons together in the courtyard of the house he had been lent. Seated before them, still weak and pale from his illness, he explained the situation.

"My mother the queen has sent a messenger asking that I return home without delay. We have no truce with the English and they are threatening to lay waste our lands. We are all needed at home, there is no doubt of that."

The barons gave quick agreement, but the king continued, "On the other hand, if we leave Acre now we give it straight into the hands of the infidels, for they would take our departure as our defeat. No Christian's life would be safe here. All must depart if we go." He paused again. "This is too great a decision to make on the instant. Come to me again in eight days and let me know how you think, my lords."

Eight days later there was another council. The barons' advice, as Louis had expected, was to return home. But John of Joinville awakened opposition.

"We canot leave Acre now," he stated flatly, "and deliver all of the poor Christians into the hands of their enemies!"

"We left Cyprus with two thousand eight hundred knights, not counting the rest of the army," said Lord William of Beaumont. "Now what do the knights number? Scarcely two hundred! We could not fight a good army of flies!"

The Count of Jaffa, who held a castle in Palestine, said quietly, "My lands are on the border here, but that is not why I speak for you to remain, Sire. I verily believe that if you can stay for a year, then the Saracens would see you mean to conquer and you would do yourself great honor. In the meantime, send for more troops."

"Troops from where?" Charles asked insolently.

"From Morea and all over the seas!" Joinville retorted. "As I have heard, my lord Louis, you have not thus far spent your own moneys but only the moneys collected for the crusade. Now spend yours for more knights! When they hear you are paying well, they will come from the ends of the earth!"

"They may be paid well, but they will not fight well," said Charles. "Even the King of France cannot buy loyalty!"

The council developed into a quarrel. The king ended the arguments.

"I have made up my mind. I shall remain."

There was an angry murmur, quickly hushed.

"Those who do not wish to stay with me are permitted to return to France with all honor. But those who do remain shall be so well paid by me, out of my own moneys, that they will be satisfied. Let it be known all over Europe that we want more knights. In this way I shall raise an army!"

The barons departed, somewhat shamefaced, and it seemed that most of them would change their minds and stay. But a few days later both of the king's brothers set sail for France, taking with them a large number of the army.

Still Louis did not complain.

"I gave them the right of choice," he said when John spoke angrily of the desertion. "Instead of thinking bitterly of those who do not agree with us, let us set our thoughts to the problem of how best to proceed. I have two aims now, John. We must free the Christian captives still held by the Saracens in Egypt, and we must fortify the towns held by the Christians here in Palestine. And then—after that . . ." The king's eyes took on the excited sparkle that had already become familiar to Joinville. "After that, John, we shall take the

Holy Sepulcher back from the infidels and re-establish the kingdom of Jerusalem!"

A few days later, Louis dispatched Lord John of Valenciennes to Egypt to negotiate for the release of the Christians still held prisoner. No sooner had the envoy departed than the Sultan of Damascus sent a message asking that the king aid him in a war against the emirs of Egypt who had killed his cousin, Malek-Moaddam. In return, the sultan would relinquish the kingdom of Jerusalem.

"Here is half of my dream dropped into my lap," Louis said when he heard the message. "And yet I cannot avail myself of it. I have a treaty of ten years' duration with the emirs. I must not break that!"

"Let us wait and see how John is received in Egypt," said Joinville. "Perhaps his demand for the release of the prisoners will be scorned. Then indeed we can join the Sultan of Damascus!"

But the emirs were surprisingly willing to listen to Lord John.

"Tell your king that if he will unite with us against the Sultan of Damascus, we will make over to him the parts we hold of the kingdom of Jerusalem," said the emir with whom Louis had made the treaty.

"That is not enough," said John.

"Then tell him also that we will cancel the debt of the two hundred thousand livres he still owes us."

"I must return to Acre to present this truce to the king," said John. "He would be more kindly disposed if you permit your prisoners to return with me."

The emir agreed. John came back to Acre with three hundred Christians who had never dreamed of tasting freedom again.

Louis thought well of the idea of becoming an ally of the Egyptians. With their forces he would indeed be able to hold his own against the Sultan of Damascus. He signed the treaty at Caesarea, which he then began to fortify along with the towns of Jaffa, Acre and Sidon. The Egyptians would come up to Gaza, the ancient seaport, while the king would gather his men at Jaffa.

But the ink was hardly dry on the treaty when the emirs and the Sultan of Damascus concluded a surprising truce and together they fell upon the city of Sidon. Almost three thousand Christians, the entire defending force, were left dead or dying when the enemy withdrew.

The king heard this news with a heavy heart. When he reached the city, a terrible sight met him. The battle had been a massacre. On the hot sandy streets, hanging out of windows, in doorways and upon the battlements where they had fallen, the bodies of men, women and children were sprawled.

Louis raised his eyes to the hot desert sky. "Father, forgive them, for they know not what they do."

Then he set the tailors and all the women to work making sacks in which to bury the dead. Quietly, often weeping, he went about with his men, lifting the mangled bodies without the slightest sign of dislike.

"These are martyrs," he reminded his knights when they turned aside, sickened. "God does not find them revolting."

Through the days it took for the burials, the word of the king's conduct spread out from the ruined city. Travelers passing on the roads, hearing of him, would turn aside to see this holy man.

"Our king is indeed a saint," Joinville said one day as he watched a dirty crew of Syrians being received with all courtesy by Louis. "The crusade may end as the others have, in failure, but for him there will be a crown of glory."

In the beginning of the year 1253 the king was at Sayette, trying desperately to convince himself and his men that the campaign was going well, when the news reached him of the death of his mother. She had ruled France with the greatest wisdom, but her anxiety over her son during his imprisonment had shortened her life. She had not been ill long. Taking the veil and making her vows as a nun at the Abbey of Maubuisson, which she had founded to be the place of her own burial, she had died on November 27, 1252.

Geoffrey of Beaulieu, the king's confessor, brought the news to Louis in the chapel tent. Louis said nothing. He knelt before the altar. After a time, Geoffrey left him. When he would have returned some time later, he was told by the bailiff that the king desired to speak to no one.

For two days Louis remained in seclusion. Then he took up the routine of his days as before, but now his knights could see that there was no youth left in him. Queen Marguerite, sending for Joinville, asked anxiously if he had seen the change in the king.

"Everyone has seen it, Madame," the knight said. "Now for the first time in his life he is completely a king. No one shares his rule."

"I share his throne," Marguerite said, and her little chin went up proudly. She was thin and there were lines of worry around her eyes. No one, not even the strongest knight, could face death as she had done in Damietta and not show the marks.

"You are indeed a queen, Madame," said Joinville, and when the tears rolled down her cheeks he added, "You do not weep for Madame Blanche, nor for yourself. Why, then?"

"I weep for my daughter Isabel who is now alone back in France. And I weep for my lord! He loved his mother above all else in this world, even above me! What will he do without her?"

"And what will France do without her?" John asked.

The barons asked one another the same question.

"Now the king must return home," the Count of Flanders said happily. He was not alone in his joy. The war appeared to be hopeless in Palestine, with the emirs and the various sultans allied with one another one day and at swords' points the next. The king had no new forces, only the remnant of the crusaders on whom he could depend. The fortifications of the towns were battered and half crumbling under the onslaught of the Saracens.

Supplies were low, the spirits of the crusaders even lower.

"We can go home in all honor," the knights said among themselves. "France needs the king now far more than does the Holy Land!"

Yet for another year the war dragged on. Finally, in the face of urgent messages from France, Louis withdrew all his knights and the women and children from Sidon and Jaffa and Caesarea, and on April 24, 1254, his fleet set sail from Acre. Two thousand vessels had left Cyprus for Egypt five years before. Thirteen galleys with mended sails and worn-out crews sailed back to France. No victory was in their hands, but they had given these years and their strength to God. Some had fallen into the sins that are induced by loneliness and the license of war; but for those who had remained good, their reward in eternity was sure.

The voyage home was perilous. Off the Island of Cyprus the *Montjoie* went aground on a sandbar with much damage to the keel. Hastily the king summoned the queen and the master mariner to him on deck.

"We may be on our way to the bottom of the sea," he told them. "Madame, awaken the children."

But Marguerite folded her trembling hands

and answered quietly, "No, my lord. Let them
go to God sleeping."

Louis was pleased. His wife had come far
in holiness since she was the silly little princess
of Provence. But he addressed the master mariner. "What shall we do, Master?"

"Leave the ship, Sire."

"There are five hundred people aboard. Will
they also leave?"

"No, Sire. There is not room for them
aboard the other galleys."

"So I save my neck while they stand in
fear of death?"

"You are of more account than us, my lord."

"We stay," said the king.

He could not be moved from his decision.
The next morning the galley was worked gently
off the sandbar and crude repairs were made to
the keel. The timbers, the master mariner
warned, might be sprung and the ship could
be parted asunder in high seas. But the king
and his family remained on the *Montjoie*.

The fleet was barely past Cyprus when a
terrible storm blew up. In the churning waves
the ships were tossed about like twigs. Surely,
the master mariner said, surely now the dam-
aged keel would part.

"Pray to St. Nicholas!" the queen begged

Joinville. "Pray! I have promised him a silver ship in memory of the miracle if he will save us!"

"I have already promised him a pilgrimage in his honor," said the knight. "I shall go from Joinville, unshod and on foot, to Varangeville to St. Nicholas' shrine as soon as it pleases God to let me!"

In a short time the wind fell, the battered sails were unfurled again and the *Montjoie* rode as well as any ship.

The next morning, Louis called all the leaders together.

"You were greatly disturbed at the showing of God's power last night," he said. "Now we must look to ourselves to see what is bad in us, for this has been merely a warning from God of the judgment to come. At any time, He can end our lives, and what is evil will remain to send us to hell. The warnings God gives us are not for His own good, for nothing good can come of them to Him. They are for our profit. Let us all, then, take care to make a good confession and from now on to live wisely."

Six weeks after setting out from Acre, the fleet came to port at Hyeres, in southern France. The king was determined not to dis-

embark until the ships reached Aigues-Mortes,
where the crusade had set sail. But after two
days of waiting, with no sign of the winds
shifting to the proper direction, he gave in. On
the third morning all the ships touched land,
and a Mass of thanksgiving was said out-of-
doors because no church could hold the great
crowd.

For five years the crusaders had been together in the great brotherhood of striving for
God. Thousands of the number had died; children had been born. The farewells were painful
among the returned travelers. But home beck-
oned, and reunion with families they had de-
spaired of seeing again. The king remained in
the city, bidding good-by to all who wished to
see him, accepting the small gifts the people
made to show their affection.

The Abbot of Cluny came with a beautiful
gift, two snow white palfreys. The next day
the abbot came again with requests to which
Louis listened with great intentness. When at
length the monk departed, Joinville, who had
been watching from a distance, approached
Louis.

"My lord, may I ask you a question?"

The king smiled. He had become very fond

of Joinville in the past years. "What is it, John?"

"Did you listen to the abbot with more attention because yesterday he gave you a fine gift?"

Louis' smile became a frown. After a long period of thought, he replied, "Yes, John, I did. Why?"

"Because then, my lord, I would say that you should bid your advisers never to take gifts from those who would ask favors, because they would surely do as you have done—listen with their minds half made up ahead of time to grant the favor."

"You are right, indeed," said the king, and he called his barons together and told them of John's advice.

"A humble man is our king," Joinville said, for he was embarrassed at all the attention his small remarks had brought.

"A saint," said the Count of Flanders.

That was the opinion of all the crusaders. In the months to follow, the fame of the saintly king would grow and become known throughout all the civilized world. The failure of his crusade would not be discussed nearly so much as his own holy way of life.

CHAPTER ELEVEN

The Cross of Red Again

Louis proceeded to Vincennes, where he remained for two days, making pilgrimages of thanksgiving to the neighboring shrines. The people of Paris, knowing their beloved king was so near, could not contain their joy. On his entry into Paris, bonfires were lighted, minstrels sang and danced in the streets, feasting and revelry went on day and night. When a week passed with no sign of the celebration's coming to an end, Louis took his family and returned to Vincennes. The money spent on frivolity, he said, could better be used to feed the poor. Hearing of this, the people abruptly stopped their merrymaking and turned their thankfulness into prayer.

The incident was to be typical of the years that followed. Word of Louis' saintliness spread as it had in Palestine. As a young man his goodness had been an example for all his subjects. Now he was not merely good, but the very light of heaven shone in his face. Every day he attended several Masses, heard the canonical hours, listened to religious discourses and instructed his children in the ways of godliness. In ruling his country he showed almost uncanny wisdom and fairness. His own vassals lived in peace under his leadership. His fame as a peacemaker was so wide that he was asked to mediate in quarrels between other countries.

During his absence many abuses of law had sprung up throughout France. One of Louis' first undertakings was to search the realm until he found men who were known for their justice. Then he gave them absolute power in the courts. The rich were favored no more than the poor, the clergy no more than the lay people. When the Pope himself asked for help in a political dispute with the King of Sicily,

who was Louis' brother Charles, Louis refused
to take part because he did not believe Charles
to be the rightful king.

Several times a week the king would go to
the woods near Vincennes, seat himself with
his back against an oak, and invite the people
who had complaints to present their claims.
Two bailiffs known for their honesty were
always with him. If the decisions of the bailiffs
did not seem fair, Louis himself would pro-
nounce the judgment. No king, the people
said, ever had ruled with the insight and honesty of Louis IX. Never had France known
such prosperity and peace.

It was a blow, then, when in 1261 there
were rumors that the king intended again to
take the cross of crusade. Surely, his subjects
protested in alarm, surely he would not leave
his country to fend for itself. There was no
Blanche of Castile now to rule as regent. Even
the saintly king, they said, could not raise an
army capable of facing the Saracens again in the
Holy Land.

All of the protests filtered back to Louis.
Troubled, he rode out to the Abbey of
Royaumont to talk with his old friend, Pacifico.
He never had recovered his strength, and he
had to be lifted from his horse by a groom.

Seated on the grass with his back against a tree he slowly regained his breath while the old monk paced in the shade. Louis never wore fine clothes any more. His tunic was of plain gray serge, his surcoat of black taffeta, and he wore no hat. Except for the beauty of his face, he could have been any peasant sitting there.

"You know what I have come to talk about, Pacifico," he said at last.

"That is so, Sire." The old man paused, his hands clasped behind him.

The king smiled. "I notice you do not urge me to go on crusade."

"I do not!"

"God gave me back my life when I was very ill, in order that I might spend it for Him."

"Then spend it in France!"

Louis laughed gently. Pacifico had not lost the peppery tongue.

"My son Philip is twenty. In another year I could see him on the throne. Then I could do what I have always yearned to do, even above my dream of crusade."

"Enter the monastery? I know," Pacifico said. "God always gives us yearnings for things we cannot do. Otherwise, we would be too contented. Christ did not care for the public life any more than you do, but He did not take the apostles and hide back in the Judean hills! No, He followed the way His Father required of Him. It is for you to do the same!"

Louis' smile had died. His white, thin hand pulled at the grass beside him.

"Bibars, who killed Robert, is now laying waste the Holy Land. Even the Templars and the Hospitallers cannot defend the holy places any more. The good man I left at Acre, Geoffrey of Sargines, writes that he cannot hold the garrison unless I send him help. Even Pope Urban has urged that I give aid with the utmost speed."

"Aid, yes," Pacifico grunted. "Send men and money, all that you can gather. For yourself, remember your mother's words: God and France!"

Louis smiled again. "You put God first, as I do."

"He desires you to share His kingship! In France!"

"I'll put crusade out of my mind for the moment, Pacifico," Louis said.

He was as good as his word. When he held a parlement at Paris that year, he did not mention a crusade. But prayers were ordered for the relief of the Holy Land, extra taxes were levied, all the young men of the kingdom were bound to certain military exercises, and extravagance in dress and entertainment was forbidden. There was no doubt that the country was in preparation for a crusade.

For the first time since Louis' return, the people were discontent. Why, they asked one another, why should they be forced into danger and expense in a foreign land when so many campaigns had already failed? The king had never recovered from the illness he had suffered in Palestine. Why should he spend his frail strength on a fruitless undertaking when he might live to reign for many years in the peace of home?

By 1263, when the crusade was openly preached, the nobles were evenly divided, some to go and some to refuse. In Lent of 1267 a summons went out to all the barons for a parlement at Paris.

Before the general meeting, Louis conferred privately with the nobles he considered to be his best advisers. The greater number agreed to join in a crusade simply because they did not wish to lose the favor of the king.

Louis knew this. That was why he asked Joinville frankly, "John, where do you stand on the subject of crusade?"

"I believe, Sire, that those who urge you to go to the Holy Land are committing a mortal sin."

The king was taken aback at the prompt answer. "Why do you say that, John?" he asked, without displeasure.

Joinville, forgetting all but his affection for the king, sat down beside him on the bench. The two were alone in the vestry of the Sainte Chapelle. Out in the body of the chapel the nobles were assembling and the priests preparing for Benediction. John laid his hand on the king's shoulder.

"Louis, I speak to you as a brother. We have grown into middle age together, shared sorrow and scant victory and defeat, and what I say comes from the heart. Last night I dreamed a dream. You knelt before the altar and upon your shoulders the priests were laying a chasuble of red serge."

"Red is the color of crusade, John."

"Yes. But the chasuble was of Reims serge, the cloth of mourning! The crusade will be of little profit, Louis! Believe me, my confessor explained the meaning of the dream and he is a man of wisdom! He knows!"

"But you will come with me as my liege man?"

"No. In my soul I know that God wants me to remain in France and look after my people. Much that was bad befell them while I was gone before. If I endanger my life again, even on so holy a pilgrimage, I should be going against God's will."

The king pressed Joinville's hand. Rising, he tottered into the sanctuary. A priest had removed the relic of the True Cross from its receptacle. Together the priest and the king faced the kneeling nobles. On the shoulders of many of the surcoats were the white crosses of accomplished crusade. Only a few wore the red of promised crusade. The king's shoulder carried no cross. Leaning weakly on the arm of a priest, he spoke with great emotion.

"My brothers, every one among you knows why I have called you together. The news from the Holy Land has become so distressing that I can no longer hesitate. All of Christendom must rise up in defense! But with the tragedy, there is also hope. The Greek Church and the Church of Rome are on the verge of reunion. And the King of Tunis has promised that if we can defend him securely against his enemies—and ours!—he and all his subjects will become Christians!"

A murmur of surprise ran over the assemblage. The king, appearing to gather strength from the very words he uttered, drew away from the priest and stood straight and tall. He held out his hand. On the palm lay a cross of red embroidery.

"Father, fasten it to my shoulder!"

The priest grew so pale he appeared to be fainting. After a long minute he folded his hands upon his breast.

"Sire, I cannot!" he whispered.

He fell to his knees. Louis looked down at the bowed head. He showed no anger. Turning to the nobles, he asked, "Who among you will affix the cross to my shoulder?"

No one moved. Slowly the king laid the cross on his own shoulder. It was of red so brilliant that it seemed to burn out over all the other light in the chapel. Then extending his arms as if they lay upon a cross, Louis raised his eyes to the beautiful stained glass window and his voice rang out.

"I have taken the cross of crusade! May God give us victory in His Holy Name!"

The king's ardor worked a miracle throughout France. Beginning in the court, where his brothers, sons, and all of his servants took the cross, the enthusiasm spread until the dissenters were only a small and nearly despised group.

But the Pope, hearing that Louis' three sons were to accompany him, wrote a letter of protest; and Queen Marguerite begged with tears that at least Philip, the heir to the throne, remain at home.

But when the crusade assembled to leave Paris, not only the sons but Princess Isabel with her husband were among the company. Marguerite was not permitted to go. Neither was she to rule as regent. The government was left in the hands of a council of regency whom the king trusted to carry on his justice.

John of Joinville, unshaken in his resolve to remain in France, had gone sadly home from the parlement; but in March of 1270 he was back in Paris for the king's departure. It was a sorrowful leave-taking. Louis, too weak to walk, was carried by Joinville to the carriage in which he would begin his journey to Aigues-Mortes. But he appeared content. The last memory Joinville would carry away was of the smile so wonderfully radiant that it seemed the king must already behold the beatific vision.

Joining the queen where she stood weeping beside the great Gate of Philip Augustus, John blinked away his own tears.

"We shall never see my lord again in this world," the queen sobbed. "He is a stubborn man. He never listened when I protested his going!"

"We say people are stubborn when they do not agree with us, Madame," Joinville said gently. "Perhaps he is right and we are wrong." His eyes were on the procession of gaily passing knights.

The queen dashed her tears away impatiently. "Where are they going, John? To Egypt? To Tunis? To Palestine? Where?"

"I do not know, Madame."

"Neither do they! And what of the ships? Will the Genoese and the Venetians send them as they have promised? And where are the provisions? Nothing is ready! If my lord ever reaches the Holy Land, it will indeed be a miracle!"

Many among the knights, reaching Aigues-Mortes, would have agreed with the queen. Companies from all over France should have been arriving at the same time, yet the king's party came alone to the city. The young knights were excited with planning, but among the older men there were quiet talks. Only their intense loyalty to the king kept the red crosses below the white on their shoulders.

Finally, on the second of July, 1270, the expedition was ready. The master mariners declared the wind to be right and the sails were set. There was singing again and praying by all the priests aboard. Now that the voyage was under way, the ardor of the young knights began to spread. Old men, hearing the stamping and neighing of the horses in the holds, were carried back in memory to the first crusade and there was much storytelling of the great victory before Damietta when Louis had seized the banner of St. Denis and waded ashore with it himself. The defeat and imprisonment which followed were not mentioned.

The king, aboard his old ship the *Montjoie*, lay on his cot and listened in silence. He seemed to be wrapped in a dream of his own, perfectly at peace. Off Sardinia a stop was made, and Louis summoned his leaders aboard the *Montjoie*. The fleet was bound, he said, for Tunis, where they would join the Mussulman prince, Mohammed Mostanser, who had promised to become a Christian. Then, with the Tunisian army, the crusaders would march on to the final conquest of the Saracens in the Holy Land.

The old knights pulled their beards. Perhaps, they said, things would go as the king declared. But opinion was divided.

"Fight the Mussulman!" said the admiral of

the fleet, Florent de Varennes. "That heathen king has no intention of giving up his gods! Show him the sword! It is the only religion he knows!"

On July 17, when the ships dropped anchor before Tunis, the admiral, strictly against Louis' orders, sent out small boats to capture the native vessels in the harbor. The nobles, believing the admiral to be in charge, obeyed his commands, and the city was taken. When Mohammed Mostanser arrived the next day, he found his army standing back from the walls and the crusaders in complete possession of the city.

Louis was bitterly disappointed. Not only did he appear to be guilty of breaking his word to the Tunisian king, but now a state of war existed. Every day, with Greek fire and battering rams and waves of foot soldiers, the enemy besieged the city. The men and provisions which were to arrive did not come. Food ran low, water was polluted, the dead lay in the streets and the cries of the wounded were pitiful to hear. Pestilence struck down those who had escaped the enemy darts, and soon the dead were no longer buried in single graves but were put into a common trench which surrounded the camp. The king's son,

John Tristram, who had been born during the sorrowful days of Damietta, fell ill and died.

The loss of his most beloved child was a terrible blow to Louis. Ridden with grief and weak in the intense heat, he visited the sick and tried to lead his men. But on the third of August, when he rose from his bed in his hot tent, he fell back fainting. He too had contracted the fever.

Word ran quickly through the camp that the king was ill, perhaps even dying, for everyone knew that in his weakened state Louis could not fight off a new sickness. The old knights shook their heads, saying nothing. Even the young knights looked at their banners snapping in the desert wind and saw the colors faded and streaked. The expedition, they said to one another, had been ill fated from the beginning, badly planned, poorly provisioned, with a leader who lived more in heaven than he did upon earth. Louis might well be a saint, but he would never go down in history as a great military strategist. And that was what the army so sorely needed now, a general to tell them what to do next. In the heat and tragedy of those August days,. all they could think about was their return home.

CHAPTER TWELVE

The Crown of Glory

FOR three weeks Louis lay ill in the hot tent. All pretense of defending the camp came to an end. In these days the enemy could have swept as easily as the windblown sand into the city of tents, but some peculiar feeling of respect for the king kept them at a distance. Small forays were made by day and night, but there was no determined attack. The crusaders' worst enemy was the pestilence. Each morning more men were counted among the stricken. And by the end of the third week, everyone knew that the king was dying.

On the morning of the twenty-fourth of August, Louis called his son Philip into his tent. The prince was only twenty. He had been eager to see Egypt and the Holy Land. Now, faced with the prospect of returning alone to rule France, he was a frightened young man. He fell to his knees beside his father's cot.

"You will not die, Father!" he protested in a choked voice.

Louis laid his hand gently on his son's head.

"Death is not a thing to fear. It is the great goal of living." Then, opening his breviary, he took out several sheets of paper filled with his own handwriting. "I have written my instructions for you, my son, in the hope that they will help you to rule as a godly king. You have been well educated in the laws of the Church and State. Remember one thing. . . ."

His voice failed and it was some time before he could continue. "Remember, my son, that I would rather have a Scotsman come from Scotland and rule our people well than to have you on the throne, a Frenchman, and rule badly."

"I will do my best, Father," the young prince promised. "But you will return to France with us!"

"My bones will go with you. Now I must

see your sister, because I cannot speak much longer."

Princess Isabel hurried into the tent with her husband, the King of Navarre, and threw herself sobbing across the foot of the bed.

Louis laid his hand tenderly on her head. "I must not keep you with me long, my dearest daughter. I have written instructions for you and for your sister, Agnes, which will lead you on in holiness. The most important is this: never lie down at night with a sinful thought, for you may go to God sleeping. Always think of how you love God, for He first loved us when we could give Him nothing, and all the love we can return will never be enough."

The king lay back, exhausted, and the three young people, overcome with grief, left the tent.

Through the day Louis lay half asleep and perfectly at peace. In the night he started up as if he were dreaming, and several times he called out, "I see Jerusalem! Let us go to Jerusalem!" When the daylight came, although he was too weak to speak, he was fully conscious, and he let his attendants know he wished to receive the Last Sacraments. They laid him, according to his instructions, beside his bed on a sack covered with ashes. Folding his hands upon his breast, he went quietly and peacefully to sleep.

At three o'clock in the afternoon, the hour when Christ expired on the cross, he woke for a moment to whisper, "Father, into Thy hands I commend my spirit." Then he closed his eyes and died.

Throughout the civilized world, even among the Saracens, there was mourning at the death of the saintly king. The *Montjoie*, bringing his bones back to France, was a funeral ship, saluted by all others it met. Half of France streamed into the small town of St. Denis, the place of burial which had been selected by Louis himself.

John of Joinville, saddened almost beyond endurance, attended the imposing ceremony and then rode out to Royaumont. In the glen where Louis had had his last interview with Pacifico, the old knight and the bowed old monk clasped hands and stood together through a long silence. Out of the chapel drifted the chanting of the brothers, a favorite passage of Louis': "Be Thou our arm in the morning, and our salvation in the time of trouble."

"Our arm in the morning," Joinville repeated. "Indeed, our king was the arm of God!"

The monk nodded.

"I was with him from youth into middle age,

and I will grow old thinking of him," John went on, "but never, if I live to the age of Methusaleh, will I recollect a single sinful act he ever performed!"

"In boyhood he was good, in manhood he was a saint," Pacifico said. "Holiness was easy for him. It was the only way he knew."

The knight strolled away to lean against the tree where Louis had sat. Looking out over the peaceful scene of the monastery fields, he gathered his thoughts, but there was no peace in his voice when he spoke.

"Pacifico, I have come to you because I can talk thus to no one else. You knew Louis well, you know me well, and you will say as you see fit." Again there was a long pause. Suddenly Joinville turned, and there was misery in his face. "Pacifico, I was not with him when he died!"

The monk seemed to have expected this. Coming slowly over to the knight, he laid his hand on his arm. "I know how you torture yourself, John. You have a tender heart. You are telling yourself in the dark hours that you should have gone with Louis to Egypt, that you were wrong in refusing so holy a man anything he asked of you."

"I told him I thought they committed a mortal sin who urged him to go!"

"You were right, John, in remaining here."

"Then the king was wrong?"

"No. He too was right." The monk came to lean against the tree. His long white beard blew across the bark and clung there. "It is the motive we must judge, John. You believed that because of the king's ill health and the difficulty he had in raising funds and an army, the crusade would come to nothing. So far as victory in the way the world knows it, it did. Nothing was gained. Many people lost their lives, much money was spent. But Louis did what he believed sincerely to be right, and so if he had done anything else, he would have been wrong."

"And for me, Pacifico?" Joinville asked.

"For you it would have been wrong to go because you believed sincerely that you could best serve God and benefit your people by remaining at home. Remember, it is a man's sincerity of motive you judge, not the outcome."

The old knight straightened his shoulders. "You put my mind at rest, Pacifico. But how could I have doubted my good king?"

"We have human doubts, John, you and I. Louis seemed to have none. He governed by the moral law and none else, and that made him a great and just king. His love of God has made him a saint. Perhaps, even in our time, we shall see him wear the crown of the canonized."

Very soon the groundwork for Pacifico's prophecy began to be laid. There were miracles, people said, taking place at St. Denis where the bones and heart of the good king were interred. Through nine centuries the ground where the abbey stood had been a hallowed spot. In the third century Denis had come north to the island in the Seine and begun preaching the gospel of Christ. The Romans, who had overrun the land of the Franks, drove him into the marshes where he continued to teach for eight years more. Then, infuriated, they hunted him out and with his hands chained but his tongue still telling the story of Nazareth and Bethlehem, he was dragged to the hill called Montmartre. The executioner's sword sent his head rolling in the dust. The people began to kick the head around like a football. Denis arose, picked it up and walked, so the legend went, to the crossroads where he lay down with his head beside him.

On this ground of the martyr's death a small church was built a hundred years later by St. Genevieve, the shepherdess who became the patron saint of Paris. Then another church rose to enshrine the first, and finally the marvelously beautiful abbey with its Gothic arches, and in it the tomb of Denis and all the other kings of France who would follow after him. His banner, the scarlet oriflamme, would be carried into battle at the head of the French army just as Louis had carried it up the Nile into Damietta and had seen it ripped and bedraggled at Mansourah. No other French king had approached saintliness. Louis IX was the first to lie in the same aura of glory as Denis.

Inside the chapel door the pilgrims looked up at the picture of Denis carrying his head, then at the new painting of Louis emerging upon these steps with the crusader's purse and pilgrim's staff he had received at this very altar. It was only proper, they said, that here, where he had been vested for his first crusade upon earth, the first miracles of his crusade in heaven should take place.

From all over France, barefooted peasants began making pilgrimages to the imposing abbey which was like a white city in itself. Noblemen, remembering the humble journeys undertaken by Louis, exchanged their taffeta and ermine for plain serge and walked barefoot with the peasants. Miracles of healing began to be reported, the lame made to walk again and the blind to see. No one was surprised. In his lifetime their king had relieved their temporal

burdens to a degree never before known. The
people rather expected him to spend his heaven-
time performing the good he could not do
when he was on earth.

His grandson, Philip the Fair, was upon the
throne when, in 1297, the cause was advanced
for Louis' canonization. Only twenty-seven
years had passed since the sorrowful day in the
hot tent in Tunis. Pacifico lay in a tomb at
Royaumont. Many others who had known
Louis were no longer living. But John of Joinville, now a white-bearded patriarch of seventy,
was summoned before the council which had
been appointed by the Pope to investigate the
life and miracles of the king, and he made a
willing but slow journey to St. Denis. For two
days he remained, answering the questions put
to him by the Archbishop of Rouen and
Brother John of Samois, who composed the
council. Then, as he had so often done in his
youth, he rode the few miles into Paris through
the gate in the white wall of Philip Augustus,
and across the Little Bridge to the Cathedral
of Notre Dame. His old eyes did not take in
the beggars on the steps or the lofty towers
or the flying buttresses spread like the legs of
a crouching spider. He was not concerned with
the present. He was living in the past of which

he had been speaking for two wonderful days, the deeply satisfying years he had spent in the company of a saint.

John remained long at prayer. He was about to rise when he became conscious of someone standing beside him. Louis had stood like that on the day they both had said good-by to Paris to start on the first crusade. But this was Marguerite, her hair as white as Joinville's beard but still carrying about her the air of expecting great things to happen. She never had quite attained what she wanted. She had been Louis' wife, the mother of eleven sons and daughters; she was the grandmother of the reigning king, Philip the Fair—but she never had been Queen of France. Blanche had not permitted it, in the beginning. Louis, later, had not trusted her judgment.

"I stood here when he spoke to me of sacrifice," Joinville said in the abrupt manner of old people. To him and to Marguerite only one person could be "he." "A sacrifice, he said, is the giving up of something good in order to gain something better. You were never Queen of France, Madame. But remembering his ways and his advice to you, you may well become a queen in heaven."

Marguerite was not disturbed by John's insight. "I came here with him every Friday to wash the beggars' feet. I did not like it. But I grew used to it. Perhaps it is a way of holiness to grow used to things."

Joinville nodded. "There are ways and ways of holiness. Once Louis asked me if I would rather be a leper or commit a mortal sin, and I replied that of course I would rather commit a mortal sin. But he told me that by one mortal sin I would cut myself off from God so completely that I could never be sure of doing enough penance to atone for it. But disease, he said, can only destroy the body. I believe that now, if he were to ask me the same thing, I would make a different answer."

The old man turned to look at the altar before which Louis had knelt so often. "I had a dream before he went on the last crusade and it came true. I knew the undertaking would not be a success. Now I have had another dream, and it will come true. I saw him in paradise, happy, laughing, and young. I spoke to him and said I would build a chapel for him at Chevillon which is not far from my castle. But he said, 'No, John, not so far away. Keep me with you.' So now I am going to dedicate to him a place in my own chapel of St. Lawrence, and if at some future time the king, his grandson, will give me a relic of the precious bones, I'll indeed have a shrine worthy of our great saint."

"The king will do as you wish," Marguerite promised. Then she pressed John's hand and went up into the vestry where she had so often accompanied Louis to wash the beggars' feet.

As slowly as he had come to St. Denis, Joinville made his way home, to spend the rest of his life thinking and writing of the saint he had known. Marguerite would still live a few years more. With her death the generation which had been close to Louis would be gone. But the king who had become a saint would never be gone from France. Cities and universities would be named for him in the old world and the new. The laws he made and the records of his justice would be patterns down through the centuries. The abbeys he built are still powerhouses of prayer, and the churches are a monument to his generosity toward God.

In the letter of advice he left for his son Philip, he wrote, "We should not fight against God with the gifts He gives us." Louis used his own gifts well. He would be mentioned in history as the leader of the dismal last crusade; but the real memory of him would remain as the great crusader for justice, law, and love of God in a time when France and the world had need of a saint.

VISION BOOKS